BREAK

By Briana Michaels

COPYRIGHT

All names, characters and events in this publication are fictitious and any resemblance to actual places, events, or real persons, living or dead, is entirely coincidental.

Dedication

For those who want double the fun—
May you be spoiled rotten and railed until you
can't walk.

Chapter 1

Six Months Ago

Nicole

"I can't keep my hands off you," Landon says, as if blown away by his own actions tonight.

I mean, none of us are acting appropriately, so I guess it is a bit of a shocker. Can you blame us? My life, future, and reputation have just been blown to smithereens in a very public way and these guys have been with me, through everything, since the beginning.

"You're so fucking perfect, Nicole." Landon kisses my neck, just above my collarbone.

He feels so good, the last of my fucks burns from the heat of his mouth on me.

Tonight, at a fundraising gala, amongst all my mutuals, celebrities, and paparazzi, I humiliated a powerful woman and got out of an arranged marriage with her son at the cost of not only my pride, but my prospects both in business and my social circle.

At least I walked out of there with my head held high and my chosen family by my side, that included my best friend Grace, Gage, and these two rebellious suit Daddies.

Leaning back into Landon, giving him more access to my body, I sway to the music and let his touch take me further into the fantasy that everything's going to be all right. That tonight wasn't as bad as I fear, and I'll wake up tomorrow better for it.

"Fuuuck, your tits are spectacular." Landon boldly cups my breasts, his touch and the heat of the dancefloor with all these bodies grinding along with the bass that's *bump, bump, bumping* makes me want to fuck.

Kerrington watches us from the bar, his eyes burning my body as much as Landon's hands are. I crook my finger at him, beckoning him to join us and he obliges, with a look that seems half amused and half suspicious.

"Do you like him groping you like that?" he asks me.

My cheeks heat when I nod, admitting what I shouldn't. Not only are we out in public being scandalous, but these two men are so off limits, it's not even funny. I don't care. All I've done tonight is make a mess of my life, so why stop when it feels so damn good?

Landon's hands go into overdrive as he skates them up and down my ribs, along my waist, and down my thighs as if he can't get enough of me. He sucks on my neck, and I stare at Kerrington while his boyfriend has his way with me. The look on his face is a mix of caution and lust. Maybe he's turned on by Landon, or maybe he's turned on by me. Or maybe, if I'm *extra* lucky, it's both of us making his dick hard right now.

My heavy lids keep my eyes barely open while Kerrington continues watching us. Our gazes lock and he brings a glass up to his sexy mouth and sips his whiskey.

Landon groans against the shell of my ear. "I'm so fucking happy you're not getting married anymore."

His words are like ice water over my head, chilling my heated body to the point that I'm almost shaking again. Then the music in the club cuts off and all the lights turn on.

Talk about a rude awakening.

"Guess it's get-the-fuck-out time." Kerrington chuckles before draining the rest of his drink. The fiery look in his gaze is gone, and he turns around to set his glass on the bar top and pays our tab.

Caught between fuck or flight, I'm buzzing from being turned on, and flooded with the urge to run from my reality. The harsh lights make me feel like I'm under a spotlight, back on stage, with everyone around me having a front-row seat to my self-destruction. I close my eyes and exhale. I'm in a club, not the gala. These strangers don't know who I am, nor do they give a shit about me. Anyone glancing at us is likely doing so because of our attire. We three are the most over-dressed ones here. My gown cost over fifty grand, and I know damn well Landon and Kerrington's suits were a pretty penny, too. Landon's a fashion slut. Honestly, I think Kerrington has gotten the most attention tonight. It's the whole dark and broody aura he gives off. Can't say I blame anyone for trying to get his number.

"Come back with us," Landon urges against my ear. He's still dancing like there's music playing. I go along with it because maybe if I pretend hard enough, the night won't be over so fast.

"Why would I do that?" I ask, coyly.

"You know why," Kerrington answers for him, suddenly back with us.

"God, I want to fuck you," Landon adds, without a care in the world. "Both of you at the same time."

My heart beats harder in my chest. I don't think Landon's ever had to filter his mouth, thoughts, or his behavior. *Must be nice.* Kerrington, however, is more guarded and unamused all the time, like me. They bring each other balance, which is wildly attractive. They don't need me in their already perfect dynamic. But…

"How bad do you want to fuck us?" I ask Landon while I stare at Kerrington.

"This bad." He grabs my hand and shoves it against his hard cock trapped in his pants. He's a big boy. A *very* big boy. My mouth waters just thinking about what he would feel like inside me.

I can't even remember the last time I had sex.

"What if Kerrington doesn't want to share?" I tease.

Landon's grin takes up his entire face. "Oh, he does. Trust me." He winks at Kerrington. "So, what do you say, Nicole? Want to keep this night going?"

The champagne buzz I've maintained all night will wear off soon, and I'm not ready for the fun to end. Because once it does, reality will hit, and I can't take it yet.

Tonight, I stood on a stage and yelled for help to get out of an arranged marriage with a man who happens to be Landon and Kerrington's best friend and business partner. Mason Finch. The media will eat this disaster up for weeks. Mason and I were never a match. And he's got someone better suited for him than I ever would be. Someone who's going to make him so fucking happy. He would never have had that with me.

I can't make anyone happy. Not myself. Not my parents. No one.

And love isn't in the cards for me—a fact I've spent most of my life coming to terms with. My parents are probably already in damage control mode, working on a new plan to match me with another wealthy man who doesn't care what his wife does as long as she's pretty, silent, and spreads her legs when she's told. The news that I'm back on the market will spread fast. Only now, my reputation is tainted, which means the respect I'll get will decline.

My heart clenches painfully. At least with Mason, I wouldn't have been used, or worse, abused. He'd have treated me like a queen and kept his hands to himself. We'd have been miserable together, and alone... together.

He got out of our horrible life tonight and dragged me out of it, too. It's for the best.

And maybe, if I prove I'm better on my own, my parents won't shove me into the arms of the next man in line.

Impossible. You know that's never going to happen.

Blood drains from my head and my knees give out a little.

"Whoa." Landon grips my waist, all playfulness gone from him as he holds me up. "Hey, are you okay?"

"I'm fine," I lie, righting myself.

Kerrington's brow furrows. "You sure?"

Tears sting my eyes, and I turn to bury my face in Landon's neck so they can't see I'm upset. "I'm thirsty and my feet hurt in these stupid heels."

His arms wrap around me like he's protecting me from the outside world. "Let's get you out of here. Kerr, get our girl some water to go."

"On it."

My heart thuds in my throat. *Our girl.* If only.

I'll never be theirs. I'll be someone else's and I'll never see these two again because I won't be allowed.

"You smell good," I say, forcing those thoughts down and clinging to the night a little longer.

Landon kisses the top of my head, and I don't even care that my hair's wet with sweat because I've danced the night away.

"Come home with us," he practically begs me. "I don't want this to end yet."

Neither do I.

Tomorrow, I'll have to face the consequences of my actions. But tonight? Tonight isn't over.

"Okay," I say, a smile tugging at my mouth.

Landon pulls back and tips my chin so I'll look at him. "Yeah?"

"Yeah." There's actual happiness in my voice and I feel a little lighter already knowing I don't have to face reality yet. "I'll come back with you."

My best friend Grace took a ride home from Gage about two hours ago. Kerrington and Landon said they were staying with me till the end, and I wonder if this was their plan all along. To get me into bed with them.

The smile on Landon's face says yes.

The one on Kerrington's says no.

Taking the water bottle from Kerrington, I add, "But only if you two really want this. It's late and I can uber home. It's not a problem."

Kerrington grabs my hand and pulls me towards the exit. "I would go insane with worry if you took an uber this late at night."

"You can always drop me off."

Kerrington halts at the door. "Nicole. Do you want to come back with us, or do you want to go home?" He waits expectantly for me to give a definitive answer, and I'm reminded of how bossy the sonofabitch can be. My pussy clenches with approval.

"She's coming with us," Landon announces, pushing the door open.

Cool air smacks my skin when I follow them outside.

"Answer me, Nicole. Stay with us or go home?" Kerrington still hasn't let go of my hand. "There is no wrong answer."

Maybe not, but there will be consequences for these actions too, and I'll be the one to pay for them. This could screw up my friendship with these two. It'll be fodder for the media if we're caught. My family will go ballistic if they find out I'm doing something like this.

But for once, I want to not care and just have fun without the weight of guilt and stress or living up to someone else's expectations.

Landon and Kerrington are a package deal.

They're offering me a night in their bed. A night of pleasure and escape. Who in their right mind would turn this down? "I want to spend the night with you both."

Kerrington arches his brow. "Are you *sure*?"

I look him in the eyes and find myself leaning into his mouth. "Yes. Absolutely."

• • •

I wake up in a haze, unsure of where I am.

Very little light filters through the curtains, but I see Kerrington's passed out on my left. All the covers are wrapped around me, exposing him to the max. His steady breathing makes his chest rise and fall while he sleeps on his back. His dick lays limp on his thigh looking all innocent and like it didn't rearrange my guts last night.

Oh my god. Last night…

Everything comes flooding back to me. The humiliating gala. Dancing at the club. Coming back to the hotel suite with Landon and Kerrington. Drinking. Kissing.

Fucking.

Oh my god… we had so much sex.

I've never been so thoroughly fucked in my life. We laughed and played and explored and every muscle I own aches. My pussy is sore in the best kind of way, and I still feel boneless and light as a feather from having both my mind and back blown.

Landon's currently in the shower. I can hear him humming a song. And since I'm in the middle of this big bed, I'm guessing he took the still warm spot on my right side all night. I was legit sandwiched between two perfect men who worshipped me for hours...

And now it's over.

God, why does that hurt so much?

The water shuts off in the shower, and panic smacks me.

Shit! I... I can't just linger. I have to go.

Slipping out of the king size bed, I quickly look around for my clothes.

Where are they? Damnit!

One heel is by the foot on the bed, the other is outside in the living room over by the balcony door. Holy hell, I remember being pressed against that glass while Landon tongue fucked me. And... I also remember Kerrington taking me from behind while I was bent over the balcony railing. The way he filled me. The way he pulled my hair and made me—

Focus, Nicole!

My dress is behind a chair, crumpled on top of a tuxedo jacket. The jacket that I squirted all over when Landon shoved the neck of a wine bottle up my—

Fucking Hell...

Adrenaline and dehydration have me shaking. I quickly slip into my dress and snag my purse off the couch. That's when a deep groan comes from the bedroom, and I hold my breath. I can't face these two this morning. Not after I took both their dicks at the same time. Not after they made me scream their names while I came harder than I ever have in my life. Not after they kissed and caressed and worshipped me afterwards in the bath and fed me chocolates and told me how beautiful I was with my mascara and lipstick smeared down my face.

Because last night was a fantasy. Today is reality.

And I need to get out of here *now*.

"Duchess, where are you?" Landon calls out in sing-songy, playfulness.

Kerrington's deep tone mumbles something I can't make out, but now I know they're both awake.

Oh no, no, no, noooo.

I trip over my own two feet as I race to the door and yank it open, only to be stopped by the heavy lock at the top. It slams so loud that I gasp. FUCKING HELL! I shut the door, unlatch the lock, and open it again, dashing for the exit before either of them can see me.

I don't do the walk of shame out of that hotel.

I fucking *sprint* it.

Heels in one hand, my purse in the other, I leave my heart in the hotel suite and run.

Chapter 2

Present Day

Kerrington

"What time is our flight?"

"Uhhhh…" Landon glances at the clock on the oven. "We've got two hours before we have to leave."

"Perfect." I slap his bare ass.

Landon cooking in nothing but an apron is a sight I'll never tire of. "Then I have time for one more round with you this morning." I bite his shoulder and untie his apron, raising it over his head.

"The eggs are going to overcook." He's wearing this gorgeous lazy grin that I've had a hand in putting on his clean-shaven face.

"I don't want eggs, anyway. Not when I can have you."

"You always say the most perfect things."

Yeah, but not the right ones, I think to myself.

Landon and I have been a little rocky ever since the night we brought Nicole to our bed. I wish I could say it was a mistake, but I can't. I loved having her there and I know Landon hasn't stopped thinking about that night, either.

That woman dashed out of our suite so fast, you'd have thought the place was on fire. She hasn't answered our calls, texts, or emails since. Her social media posts have changed too, which makes me think someone else is running her accounts now. It's like she's avoiding not just us, but the whole world.

I've asked Mason a couple times if he's heard from her, but when he asked why I was so curious, I made up some nonchalant reason and never brought it up again.

Landon turns the burner off and abandons breakfast, ready to lure me back to one of our bedrooms.

"No." I pull him back to me. "Here."

He arches a brow and licks his lips. "Okay." Then he goes down on his knees and starts unbuckling my dress pants.

"No." I tug him up. "I want you on the counter."

His brow twitches with confusion for a second, but he climbs up and waits for my next orders.

The nice thing about Landon is he's up for anything.

His dick is at half-mast, so I stroke it to attention while keeping my gaze locked on his. Then I lean down and take him into my mouth.

"Oh fuuuuuck," he groans quietly.

Holding his base, I lick his shaft and playfully suck on the tip.

"You feel so good, Kerr."

Keeping my pace steady, I suck him off like I've got all the time in the world. I love making Landon feel good. I love taking care of him.

And I love making him beg.

"I want to come," he whimpers, then groans again when I stroke him with a tighter grip.

"Not until I say you can."

He bites his pouty bottom lip and leans back, breathing harder as he holds his control for me like a good boy. I tease and punish him until I know he's vibrating with the need to blow.

I look up at him and wink, giving him silent permission to unload in my mouth.

Three strokes later and he's roaring his release, his hand in my hair, fucking it up while he rides his pleasure wave. Once I've swallowed my breakfast, I lick my lips and grab my waiting coffee from the counter.

Landon hops down, looking dazed and confused. "What was that for?"

I shrug and take another sip, not telling him why. It's not like I need a reason to pleasure him, just like he doesn't need one to with me. We're just...

Hell, I have no idea what we are anymore.

"Come here," he says playfully, going for my belt again.

My firm hand over his stops him. "Not

now."

The happy, blissed out look he's wearing fades in a blink. Replaced by rejection. "Why not?"

I turn to leave because I'm not ready for this conversation, and quite frankly, I don't think he is either. "I'm going to shoot some emails off before we have to go."

His stare burns into my back, and I ignore it.

By the time I'm in the living room of our condo, he's banging pots and dumping our half-cooked breakfast into the trash. Then he storms past me and heads to his bedroom, slamming the door shut.

It makes my stomach drop every time he gets like this because I know one day he'll walk out the door and never come back.

I'm not enough for him.

Even when I try to be… I'm not.

I think this trip will be a tipping point for our… situationship. We're spending the week with Mason and Leah to go over some business shit for her company, the Brazen Bunny, and also have some fun. Honestly, Landon and I have been working like dogs for months. I think the stress of work has added unnecessary pressure to our relationship too.

Thank God we've finally both walked away from BanditFX. He left with Mason when the company was sold off about seven months ago, but Gage and I stayed on the board to make sure things transferred smoothly. I thought it would have taken longer to get everything in order, but we were too efficient for our own good, I guess.

Now Landon and I are floating in this weird in between space, both professionally and romantically. Landon started helping Leah with her online business, and I've been eager to get more involved myself, but every time I try to help with the workload, he says he's got it handled.

He's hella smart and just as savvy as I am, if not more, but damn, when he rejects my assistance, it still hurts. I think he's using the Brazen Bunny project with Leah as a distraction from Nicole. Not that I blame him for needing something to occupy his mind. Technically, we made so much off selling BanditFX, that neither of us have to work a day in our lives anymore, but I love a challenge of a new project, and Landon would be bored out of his mind without something to keep him busy. Besides, one can never have too much money. If we can work out this integrated payment platform for Leah's new company, we can offer it to others and make a mint again.

But money won't buy us the one thing I think we both need.

Nicole.

My gaze drifts to Landon's door again. I hate when he's upset, and I keep screwing things up between us.

How do I tell him how I feel without losing

him? How am I supposed to make things right when they've been a little wrong since the very beginning?

A tension headache forms, and I shut my laptop, abandoning work all together. Shoving my gear into my waiting backpack, I fold the blanket on our couch, straighten the chairs, water the plants, and wipe down the kitchen sink. None of this mundane bullshit helps take my mind off Landon.

I don't like tension between us, damnit.

Creeping to his door, I press my ear against it and listen.

"If you're going to hover, you might as well join," he grumbles from inside.

Well shit, I didn't think he'd notice me out here.

Popping my head in, I see him lying on his bed, dressed in a pair of jeans and a Henley that fits him like a glove. He's holding his phone with one hand, the other tucked behind his head.

"She's got a new post," he says.

I gave up on stalking Nicole online months ago. Landon, however, seems to have made it part of his daily routine. I don't know how I feel about that.

"What's it about?" I ask, against my better judgement. "New business collab, or another ploy for donations to the Greystone Foundation?"

Those are the only kinds of posts she makes on social media. Because she's tied so tightly to her family's well-known corporation, and since she doesn't mix business with pleasure, Nicole never posts personal stuff online. Ever.

"It says she's stepping away and taking a break. There's a link to mental health awareness added to it."

My heart crashes.

We stare at each other, both rocking huge concerns, and I'm already pulling out my phone, dialing her number.

Of course it goes straight to voicemail. And the inbox is full.

Fuuuuck.

"This is bad," Landon says.

And there's a part of me that takes the blame for it.

The morning she left our hotel suite, the first article published online about the gala. Then another. Then another. It wasn't enough to make international news, but it definitely made the rounds in every part of the judgmental society she's part of.

Greystone heiress rejected by Big Tech Heartthrob.

Nicole Greystone publicly dethroned by Camgirl.

The click bait got uglier and uglier from there.

Greystone Princess rebels with ex-fiancé's best friends.

Rebound and Reboot- Taking revenge where she

can find it.

But everything went away before it had a chance to go viral. Mason told us her family likely paid off the reporters to have them take their pieces down, or perhaps threatened to sue them.

It was a whirlwind mess that lasted less than seventy-two hours online but has become immortal in my brain. Landon's too.

"This fucking sucks." He tosses his cell on the bed. "I can't believe she's shut us out. We didn't do anything wrong."

"Her family controls her, Lan. You know that."

"She's a grown woman, for fuck's sake."

True, but we learned from Mason how their families are. It's terrifying, honestly. "Mason was a grown man," I remind him.

"Yeah, and he got out of all that. He broke the cycle."

"Maybe she's trying to do that now, too."

One can only dream, right?

Landon runs a hand through his wavy dark blond hair. "If she'd just let us help her."

Silence falls, and I clench my teeth. I'm constantly pulling myself back from going off the deep end with my thoughts because it never helps. I've worried about her for so long, it's become second nature.

The only reason I haven't kicked down her door, or showed up at her office, is because I don't want to make things worse for her. Not after all those goddamn bullshit headlines.

I also don't want Landon to think I'm not happy with him anymore. There's been this guilt-ridden strain on our relationship ever since that night and I hate it. To make it worse, there's this awful, invisible elephant in the room that neither of us has had the balls to acknowledge.

I'm hiding something from him. And I suspect he's hiding something from me.

His cell buzzes and I think we both have an irrational burst of hope when we hear it. Landon snatches it fast and frowns. "Our driver will be here in five minutes," he says, resting his head back on his pillow again.

"Okay. I'll do another sweep, then we can head downstairs." Backing out of his room, I check the stove, iron, and a bunch of other things I know are already turned off. When Landon comes out carrying his duffel, I grab my backpack and open the door for him.

"Maybe Mason will know something." Landon looks expectantly at me for hope.

"Maybe." I smile, but it feels foreign on my face.

Taking his hand and squeezing it, I give him a little reassurance. When he returns the favor, that's all I need to know that, for another day, we're going to be okay.

But what about tomorrow?

Chapter 3

Landon

The flight was uneventful and Kerrington and I only make small talk before and after the inflight movie. When we land, I hand him his bag, grab my own, then we silently walk out of the airport and straight to Mason's waiting car.

"Hello boys," Leah says with this massive smile on her face. "Miss me?"

"Getcha ass over here, woman!" My heart pounds with excitement at just seeing my girl, Leah. She runs over and jumps into my arms, wrapping her legs around me, and squeals when I twirl her.

I'm so fucking happy for Mason because he's found his missing piece. Every man deserves a Leah in their life and I'm damn grateful she's in mine too.

"Kerrington," she says in a flirty tone once I let her go.

"Leah." He easily wraps her in a warm hug.

God, I love how he does that. His embrace, whether it's with me or someone else he cares about, is all-encompassing. Like it's folding you into armor or some shit. Makes you feel safe and cherished.

My mind flashes back to when he held Nicole close to him that one amazing night. He's hugged her a million times, but six months ago he held her exactly like this—like he wanted to keep her. Tuck her into his pocket and save her for later.

That was the best night of our life together. We both got what we needed for the first time in forever. And by morning, it was gone. Vanished. As if it had never been.

As my Dom, Kerrington makes sure all my needs are met… when he can. And the fact that he can't fulfill all of them makes our connection glitchy at best some days. He's trying. I know that. But I don't think I'm enough for him either, which makes me feel some kind of way.

I *need* Nicole. That's the bottom line.

I need Nicole and Kerrington *both*, which breaks my heart because I can't have one, and I'm sure to lose the other, eventually.

With Nicole now going on some kind of social media hiatus, the only link I had left to her has been severed. At least when I kept up with her posts, it was like I could pretend we were back in the good old days. It's not like Nicole and I talked much outside of social gatherings, so keeping up with her online has always been part of my life. Even in college. I just never told anyone about it. And now it's gone.

Actually, it's been gone for a while, considering all her damn posts are of other people and not her. Or, if she is in it, she's so far away, or in the back of the group photo, that I can't get a good look at her. It drives me nuts.

And Kerr and I have been so rocky lately, I'm scared that the one night with Nicole has destroyed us. I can feel him pulling away from me more and more, and I'm doing the same. It's not that I don't love him, because fuck yeah, I do. It's just that I can't bear the thought of not being enough for him. And I know he's not enough for me.

Christ, I'm an asshole.

It's just that a person can't thrive off tiny bites of food every day. They need whole, well-balanced meals. Landon and I are not well-balanced and never truly have been.

"What's up with you two?" Leah asks, breaking me away from my thoughts.

"Long night and an early flight," Kerrington says with a tired smile. "We're beat."

"You look it," Mason teases.

Flipping him the bird, I walk over and give him a hug. "It's good to see you, man."

We all climb into Mason's car and Leah buckles up first. "You guys hungry?"

"Starved," I say from the backseat.

Kerrington groans, dramatically. "Step on it, Mase. None of us can survive a hangry Landon."

So true.

Leah looks back and waggles her eyebrows at me. "There's a new place I've been dying to try that apparently makes the best, fattest, juiciest burgers. Wanna go there?"

"As if you have to ask?"

I place my hand over Kerrington's and sigh heavily.

I'm tired. Frustrated. And also relieved. The mix of emotions only makes me want to eat my feelings, so a big ass burger sounds perfect.

• • •

After devouring a meal that could feed a family of five, I'm feeling way better. We can't check into our hotel for another couple of hours, so we're heading to Mason's place.

"I don't know why you two don't just stay with us," Leah pouts.

I grin like a devil. "You don't?" We climb out of the car, and I whisper in her ear, "We break headboards, baby. I'm not about to smash up your furniture on night one."

She howls with laughter and high fives me.

Gage, Mason, and Leah all know Kerrington and I are a thing. We fucked around a bit in college and had some occasional fun after we got BanditFx going. Long nights in the office were perfect for us to slam together and get our pent-up energy out. We finally took things to the next level and moved in together two years ago. Even though we have separate bedrooms, I'm usually in his bed every night, anyway.

We've occasionally invited others to join us. Always a woman. Nicole was the last one and honestly, I don't think I can move past it.

She was the perfect fit for us.

Kerrington isn't a switch like me, and he understands the importance of needing a sub because he has me to fill that role for him. Which means he might also understand, especially after that incredible night with Nicole, that I need the same fucking thing, although I haven't admitted that part out loud. I thought maybe it was a blip. A little itch I could scratch to get it out of my system.

Nicole is *not* a woman you get out of your system. And the desire to get back what I had that night isn't something I can turn off. Not easily, at least.

Mason hooks his arm around Leah's waist and escorts her inside. Kerr and I follow.

"What do you guys want to do today?" I ask, eager to have some fun. See? I'm such a happy boy after I've eaten. "Movies? Shopping? Board game? Ohhh Monopoly?"

"You're not allowed to play Monopoly," Kerrington reminds me with a sharp tone. "Remember the snowstorm blood bath from four years ago?"

Mason visibly shivers. "God damnit, now

I'm going to have nightmares again."

"That bad?" Leah laughs.

"Princess, you have no idea." Mason shoves an accusatory finger at me. "That man looks like a golden retriever, but he's a shark. A nasty, greedy, take it all shark."

Holding my chest, I gasp. "That's not true. I'm just better at getting what I want than the rest of you."

"You're a monster," Kerrington tosses out there.

"I prefer the term Shameless Entrepreneur."

"He'll take everything from you with a smile on his face," Mason explains to Leah.

She shrugs. "Well, isn't that how you play to win?"

"Exactly. See? She gets me." I hook my arm around hers and pull her away from Mason. "I'd never do that to you, though. You're my favorite."

"Don't believe him, Leah!" Kerrington warns from behind us. "He's a fucking menace with no conscience."

Eye-rolling dramatically, I lean into her. "He's still scarred about going bankrupt after three turns around the board." I cluck my tongue. "Really, Kerrington, grow a pair and fight me for Broadway next time."

We take the elevator up to Mason's condo and when the door opens, it's like I step into a dream.

No.

It's a nightmare.

"Nicole?" Mason's voice fills with alarm. "What the fuck are you doing here?"

She takes one look at me and collapses.

Chapter 4

Kerrington

My instincts propel me forward and I nearly catch Nicole, but Landon beats me to it.

"Jesus Christ, what's happened to her?" My heart is in my throat as I stare at the woman I've obsessed over for far too long. She's lost weight since we last saw her. There are dark circles under her eyes and her cheeks are hollow. Even her hair is dry and thin.

"Get her on the couch," Mason barks.

Leah dashes to the kitchen and comes back with water.

Landon carefully rests Nicole on the couch but doesn't let go of her. "Hey," he says gently, trying to coax her awake. "Come on, baby. Wake up for us."

Leah hands me the glass of water and now me and Mason are both on either side of Landon, all on our knees, trying to wake her up.

Nicole's eyebrows twitch. "Mmph."

"Duchess," I say in a more authoritative tone. "Open your eyes for us, please."

Landon spares me a glance that burns with

annoyance, and then he focuses back on her.

Nicole finally comes to and the first person she looks at is Mason. "Ugh." She groans, pushing him back with her hand on his face. "Too close, Mase."

Leah sighs with relief. "Well, she's back to normal, at least."

"God damn, woman." Mason rises to his feet and huffs. "You scared the shit out of us."

She doesn't respond. Instead, she looks at Landon and tears well in her eyes.

I'm eager to do anything it takes to make that look go away. "Here," I shove the glass of water in her hands. "Drink this."

Nicole doesn't obey me.

"Drink it," Landon says in a calmer tone. "You'll feel better."

She still doesn't listen.

"Duchess, so help me god, I'll pry your mouth open and pour it in if I have to."

"Landon!" Mason barks.

But she takes the glass and drains half of it before handing it back to me.

"Good girl," Landon and I say at the same time.

Memories of our one night together bang on the door of my mind, but I don't open it. I refuse to revisit the best night of my life. Not now. Not when she's looking so rough and beat down.

"Give me a minute." She pushes her way through the barrier Landon and I have made with our bodies.

Leah helps Nicole into the bathroom and talks in a voice too quiet for us to make out what she's saying.

Mason drops onto the couch and scrubs his face. "I should have known this would happen."

"The fuck does that mean?" Landon asks with a possessive edge to his voice.

"Ever since the night of the gala," Mason says, "she's been running herself into the ground. Looks like things have finally caught up with her."

Nicole works for her family's company. They take over businesses that are floundering or close to bankruptcy and figure out if they're worth saving or will buy them out and basically tear the corporation down. In her "spare time", if you can actually call it that, she does heavy philanthropy work around the world.

"Why didn't you say something about this sooner?" Landon asks, angrily.

"Why would I?" he counters. "It's not like you can do anything for her."

I think Landon and I both feel the stab from that remark.

"Besides," Mason continues. "I've been trying to help her as much as possible, especially since that blow up at the gala was all my fault, but she won't listen to reason. She fucking blocked me on everything."

She blocked him, but not us? She just

ignores us. I can't tell if that's better or worse.

Landon frowns. "Why would she be so stubborn?"

"Because that's all that woman is," Mason grumbles. "She doesn't listen for shit. No one can tell her what to do."

That's… not the experience we've had with her. Our girl listens extremely well when you use the right incentives. Suddenly, the door in my mind rips off the hinges and the memories of our night together come flooding in…

"Take his cock in your mouth, Duchess."

Nicole drops to her knees and looks up at Landon with her pretty lips parting as she does as I command. The minute her lips wrap around his dick, Landon's head tips back and he lets out this beautiful groan.

"That's it. Suck him off. Look how good you make him feel."

He threads his fingers in her thick blonde hair and looks down at her again. "Such a good girl." His hips pump faster until she's slurping and gagging. "Listen to those noises, Kerr. Our girl enjoys teasing us."

She gets even louder.

"Want us to fuck you, Duchess?" Landon slows his thrusts. "One hole for me, one hole for Kerrington. We can fill you up, baby. Is that what you want?"

Nicole pulls off and licks her lips. "Yes. God, yes."

"God is not my name tonight," Landon reminds

her, cocking his brow. *"Try again."*

"Yes, Trick."

For the first time ever, I see that he's needed to be a Dom to a complete submissive. Something in me cracks. Landon once told me he was a Switch, but any time we brought a woman to our bed, he's never Dommed her. I've called all the shots, every time. Tonight, I'm seeing Landon take the reins and... I fucking love the way he looks doing it.

I want him happy. I want him satisfied.

I want him.

My dick hardens to the point of pain. Landon looks over at me and sees me jerking off. "Like the view?" he asks, his gaze beckoning me to join them.

I close the gap between us and kiss Nicole first. She's so soft and sweet. Then I grab Landon by the throat and kiss him. His mouth opens for me and he's rougher and stronger than our gorgeous Duchess. It's like I get to have a taste of two different worlds and they're both addicting.

"I want to fuck you first." I keep my hand collared around his throat. "While you fuck her."

Landon's eyes roll at the thought of the pleasure this promises. "Okay." Then he turns his gaze to our lovely girl still waiting on her knees. "Get on the bed, Duchess."

She crawls across the room and climbs into our hotel bed. With her hands on the headboard, she looks over her shoulder at us and smiles.

"Fucking hell," Landon whispers.

I kiss his shoulder. "Looks more like heaven to me."

We both go for her, worshipping, caressing, and preparing one another for what's about to happen.

When we line up, she faces the headboard and grips it tight. "Don't go easy on me, Trick."

"Trust me, I won't." Landon smacks her ass while I lube up behind him…

Landon's blue eyes lift to mine. "Why didn't she call us?"

"Why should she?" My tone is probably more defensive than necessary. "It's not like she's ours."

The minute I say it, I feel the loss of her disappearing that morning like a fresh fucking wound.

The best night of my life was followed by shame and regret. We both heard her escape. As if she couldn't get out of our hotel room fast enough. As if being with the two of us was so damning, so embarrassing, so horrible, she couldn't stand to be in the suite with us for another second.

Mason sighs and looks in the direction that Leah and Nicole have gone. "Nicole's suffocating, trying to please everyone around her."

"Who the fuck does she have to please other than herself?" Landon asks incredulously.

"Her parents. Her peers. The media. Her competition." Mason frowns. "I got out of our circle of Hell, but she's still caught in the middle of it. I keep trying to help her, but she's not willing to let me."

My feet are moving before I have enough sense to see reason. I march down the hall and bang on the door. "Let me in, Nicole."

"No," she shoots back, and I can hear the strain in her voice. It makes me ten times more protective of her.

"Duchess, please let us in." Landon's by my side, his hand pressed against the door. "We just want to talk with you."

It swings open. "Don't you dare call me Duch—"

I'm shoving my way inside, making her back up as I go, before she can finish that sentence.

Landon's on my heels. "Leah, give us a minute, okay?"

She leaves, biting her bottom lip, and closes the door with a soft click.

I don't take my eyes off Nicole. My entire body locks because I'm torn between instinct and common sense.

Her chin trembles, eyes red-rimmed and bright. She swipes the tears off her cheeks and her ring spins on her finger because it's too fucking loose. She's a shell of the woman we know.

"Come here, baby." I close the space between us and wrap my arms around her. The instant I do, she crumbles. Her body sags against me and it's like she finally gives up whatever fight she's been in.

The entire bathroom seems to hold its breath. I let her cry against me until her sobs fade and she's taking in deep, shaky breaths.

Landon and I look at each other while she remains buried in my arms and I'm at a complete loss. I see the longing on his face and feel the desperation in her hands as she clings to my shirt and suddenly, I only have one purpose in this life.

"Landon." I keep my tone calm. "We have a change in plans."

"Yeah, we definitely fucking do."

I scoop her into my arms and carry her out of the bathroom.

Then I march right out the goddamn door.

Chapter 5

I came to Mason and Leah's for a break from the madness in my life.

I'm leaving it in the arms of the man responsible for my madness.

Okay, that's not fair. Kerrington isn't solely to blame, because Landon had a hand in it too.

And yes, I'm fully aware that I'm also at fault because I consented to going home with them and submitting completely that night, six months ago, and *nothing's* been the same since.

Fuck, my chest feels too tight.

"I'll drive," Landon announces with an edge to his tone. He sounds mad, and that makes me feel worse.

We get into my car and the engine roars to life. I'm too tired to even care how they got my car key or that I'm letting them take me away like this. Instead of sitting up front with Landon, Kerrington is in the back seat with me, keeping me in his lap. I feel like a big baby and shame hits me in the throat.

I've avoided both of them for months and

now I'm right back where I shouldn't be.

My problems started that night of the gala when I fucked all my prospects of marriage by going to the club, getting caught up in a fantasy, and having the greatest night of my life with the very two men who've haunted my dreams. And now they're driving me away from Mason and Leah's, taking me. "Where are we going?"

I wish I actually cared.

"To our hotel." Landon glanced at me from the rearview mirror.

"Unless there's some other place you'd prefer?" Kerrington adds.

I stay silent because I can't think straight anymore.

The past month has been the hardest of my career. I finally had to tap out, which is why I came to Mason and Leah's. They said I could stay with them if I ever reach my breaking point, or if I needed an escape, and Mason gave me a key to their condo just before I blocked him from everything.

He's been cut out of our society and all the toxic bullshit that comes with it, so his place is an oasis that I will never have for myself. I feel bad for blocking him, but it was the only thing I could think of to keep him out of my bullshit.

Anger stirs in me whenever I think of how unfair all this is.

Mason walked away from our toxic society with a clean break, and I'm still swirling in a vortex of proving myself capable to everyone. I'll never hate him for getting out of this life. He earned it. And he's been trying to take me with him ever since. I just wish I knew how to do what he did. No business venture I come up with is good enough for what I want in my life, and the failure stings. Meanwhile, I'm the shark circling companies that are bleeding out, and I devour them on behalf of my family's business. It's not easy to look in the eyes of men who are begging for financial help and you have to not only deny them, but have them sign over their companies that we will break down and tear apart. It's like running a corporate chop shop in my mind. And to say it's not personal, it's business? What a crock of shit.

It's personal to them. And the anger I face, the resentment I endure is too much some days.

We pull into a drive thru and I don't answer either of them when they ask what I want to eat. I'm too nauseous to think about food. Landon orders a bunch of random combo meals and I just stare out the window. Then I finally slide off Kerrington's lap and hug myself.

I shouldn't be here.

"Buckle up," he orders.

I deftly reach for the seatbelt and click it in place.

"Lay your head back and close your eyes."

As I do what Kerrington tells me, I feel a warm weight settle on my chest and lap. Cracking my eyes open, I see he's put his jacket over me like a blanket. It smells like him. It still holds his body heat. The scent of greasy burgers and fries fills the car, and Landon tears off down the road again.

For the first time in a long while, I feel at ease and sleep takes me.

• • •

"Come on, baby."

My eyes fly open when the warm jacket is pulled off my lap and, for a second, I can't figure out where I am or how long I nodded off. "What's going on?"

"We're at the hotel." Landon calmly unbuckles my seatbelt and lifts me out of the vehicle.

"I can walk."

"I know." He scoops me up and tightly holds me against him. "Indulge us, Duchess. Let me take care of you."

Over Landon's shoulder, I watch Kerrington grab my bag and the food from my car before handing my key to the valet. The attendant won't stop staring at me with pity, either.

Tears well in my eyes. I look so weak. This is embarrassing. "Put me down."

"Duch—"

"Put me down!"

Once my feet gently hit the ground, I fix my

shirt, annoyed at everything. That nap in the back seat felt like a hundred years and a blink, and now I'm dizzy and wired. What a clusterfuck.

Kerrington heads to the reception desk, I guess to check in.

"What are you guys doing here?" I ask Landon.

He's quiet for a heartbeat and then says, "Kerr and Gage settled everything that was left at BanditFX, so we came to see Mason and hopefully get this new project underway with Leah so we can bring it to a few other waiting clients."

Jealousy coils in my belly. Whatever they're doing will hit big, I have no doubt. Things come so easily for Mason and his friends. If it was just about putting in the hard work, I'd be an independent millionaire myself too, but it's not enough.

Nothing is enough.

Kerrington returns with two key cards and hands one to Landon. "We're in the penthouse."

Of course they are. Nothing but the best for these guys.

"Let's go." Landon sweeps his arm towards the elevator, and I follow them in silence. When we get inside and the door closes, my stomach rumbles loudly. Landon snags the bag of food from Kerrington and roots around, pulling out a fry. "Open."

I glower at the fry he's got up to my lips.

"Open, Nicole."

I'm not a trained circus lion, for fuck's sake. So why do my lips part so he can place the fry in my mouth?

Who cares? It's salty and tasty and I'm starving. "Can I have another?"

"Absofuckinglutely." Landon quickly pulls out two more and feeds them to me.

I close my eyes, chewing while leaning against the back of the elevator. The door eventually opens to a long hallway. Their suite is at the end, and I take a lifetime to walk there on my own. The guys don't rush me either.

Kerrington escorts me inside. "Were you planning on staying at Mason's?"

"Yes."

"You're staying with us now."

His words land like an anvil at my feet, bolting me down. I've known these guys for years. Whenever Mason's friends come to New York, we eventually run into each other because Mason and I ran in the same social circles. I've always envied Gage, Landon, and Kerrington because they weren't from my and Mason's world. They were outsiders. New money. Young money.

Most of our families looked down on them because of it.

I, however, saw them as idols. Not because they were rich. Hell, I have plenty of my own money. It's that they don't care about what others think of them. Landon legit ordered Door Dash at a ten-thousand dollar a plate fundraiser and ate it with the biggest smile ever while the room gawked and talked shit about him.

Kerrington isn't much better, he's just more subtle about it.

To live a carefree life and not worry about what everyone else thinks of you is foreign to me. I got a taste of it that night in the club. I danced my ass off, laughing and drinking with two hot as fuck men. I went back to their hotel and submitted to them. Begged for their cocks. Was a whore on my knees. Curled in their laps like a kitten. Rode their dicks like a jockey. Took them both at the same time and let them come all over me. Inside me.

For one night, I wasn't Nicole Greystone. I wasn't the good daughter who makes her parents proud. I wasn't even the friend who put on a mask and acts like everything's great, like when I'm with my bestie Grace.

I was someone else. Someone I'm scared of. Because if my truth got out, I'd be finished. Ruined. And I can't claw my way back from that level of destruction. Jesus, even the one-night stand I had with these two wrecked my reputation enough that my parents have barely spoken to me in months.

Do you know how horrible it feels to work for someone who will look through you like you're fucking cellophane when they used to regard you with pride and joy?

My eyes sting with tears again. You'd think I'd cried all the water out of my body at this point. And it's clear I haven't learned my lesson, because here I am, right where I do not belong again.

"Sit her on the couch," Kerrington orders. "Quick."

It's only when I feel Landon hoist me up I realize my knees have buckled.

"Jesus Christ, Nicole." He carries me over to the enormous sofa and carefully sets me on it. "When was the last time you ate?"

I blink slowly, trying to remember. I come up with nothing because my head is too cluttered. "Maybe… I don't know… a smoothie… on Sunday."

Landon's gaze cuts to Kerrington. His jaw clenches and eyes tighten.

"Sunday was three days ago," Kerrington says out loud.

I nod.

"Oh my fucking God." Landon retrieves the bag of food and dumps it all out on the coffee table. Quickly unwrapping a burger, he holds it up for me to take. "Eat this." When I stare at it, he grows mad. "*Now*, Duchess."

It's the honorific that sets me into action. My arm feels like it weighs a hundred pounds as I reach out for the burger and take it from him. I nibble on it in silence, dreading that this will eventually turn into an interrogation of some kind. I don't want to tell them what's wrong with me. I don't want to admit it.

"Drink." Kerrington unscrews the cap off a bottle of water and hands it over.

I get down three bites of the burger before feeling nauseous again. "My stomach hurts."

"Okay." Landon's voice is so soft and kind. "Here." He takes the burger from me and Kerrington quickly grabs a trash can, placing it between my feet in case I puke.

"We've got you." Landon sits down next to me and gathers my hair back. "You're going to be okay, sweetheart."

No. I'm not.

Chapter 6

Landon

Never in my life have I felt more helpless than right now. A million horrifying possibilities race through my mind for what could cause Nicole to look and act like this.

She's withering away. This strong-willed, brilliant, cunning, independent bombshell is…

"Are you sick? Have you… been diagnosed with something?"

Jesus, what if she has cancer? Or some rare disease that they haven't identified yet?

Nicole shakes her head and sips the water. Hoping she's not actually going to yack up her meal, I let go of her hair and rub her back instead.

Kerrington squats down in front of her and places his hands on her thighs. "What's going on, Nicole? Please talk to us."

Her sweet chin trembles and she shakes her head, not answering more than that.

She'll share when she's ready. Or maybe we'll never know. Nicole doesn't owe us anything, least of all an explanation for her current state. But it's obvious neither Kerrington nor I will let her leave here tonight. Shit, if I had my way, she'd never walk away from us again.

Nothing's been the same since our one and only night together, and I'd give anything to turn back time.

I want to take care of this woman. I think Kerrington does too. Not that we've ever really discussed our feelings or desires much. He and I? Well, we just go with the flow. Only lately it's been less flow and more like white water rafting.

"Landon, run our girl a bath."

My stomach does a weird twist when he orders me in that tone of his. I don't always like it and I sure as shit don't need to be bossed around in a moment like this. Still, I get up and follow his orders because I want desperately to take care of her, and Kerrington is extremely good at taking care of me so… I guess he's just used to calling all the shots.

Getting the tub ready, I make sure it's perfect. Bath salts, dim lights, some lavender oil. This suite has everything one needs to be pampered like a bougie bitch.

It's me. I'm a bougie bitch.

It wouldn't surprise me at all if Kerrington called ahead and had all my favorites delivered ahead of time to our suite. He's thorough and thoughtful like that.

The man's perfect.

Guilt makes my hands clammy. What the fuck are we doing? Not just today, but…

"Almost there," he says from the doorway,

helping Nicole walk.

Is she so fucking weak she can barely hold herself up? What's happened to her, goddamnit? The worst part about this is I *like* that she's become this helpless. I said what I said. I don't want her to suffer, but if hitting some kind of rock bottom is what's brought her back to us, I'm grateful.

I'll burn in Hell later for that when the day comes, but it won't be today.

"Just a few more steps," he encourages. "I'm so proud of you, Duchess. You're doing great."

Duchess.

We gave her that nickname the night we shared her together. Actually, I gave it to her, and I told her to call me Trick. It made the things we did that much more fun because we weren't ourselves. I got to be someone I've always wanted to be, and Nicole didn't have to be Nicole.

I saw the way she responded to it earlier today, too. Her eyes sparked a little. Or maybe I'm delusional.

Tabling that thought, I help her out of her clothes. My heart stutters to a stop when I see her ribcage. She's lost too much weight. Fucking hell.

"I've got it," she snaps, when Kerrington tries to unclasp her bra.

He puts his hands up in surrender and backs away.

With her gaze cast to the marble floor, she slips out of her bra and panties and climbs into the soaking tub with my guided help. Christ, her hands are icy. "Easy, baby. Don't slip."

She finally settles into the water and sighs, looking relieved and exhausted.

"Kerr, go order our girl some chocolate and more water. And tea. Jasmine green tea."

After he slips out of the bathroom, she looks up at me with her gorgeous hazel eyes. "How did you know I like jasmine green tea?"

I know a lot about Nicole, actually. Probably too much, considering my best friend Mason was her betrothed for years. Even though they've always acted like they can't stand each other, he's been there for her, which means so has Kerrington, Gage and I. Leah now, too. Nicole's part of our rebellious family. She just doesn't see it that way yet.

Kerrington's deep voice echoes from outside as he orders room service, then he peeks back in. "You want chocolate mousse or a box of chocolates?"

"Both," I answer before she can. It's a dick move, but I'm too riled up and my possessive instincts have taken control. "And send someone out for those thin mint candies we get with the bill at Marcellos in Manhattan."

Yeah, I've gone off the deep end now. But they're her favorite, and so help me God, I'll fly to New York myself tonight if I have to, just to go to that restaurant and get them if that's what it takes to make her feel better.

"How did you—" Nicole huffs a little laugh and shakes her head. "You're crazy."

For you, I wish I could say, but I'm not trying to sound like a douche. Besides, I'm too awestruck by the smile she's finally got on her face.

"I've missed you," I blurt out. "Why'd you leave us that morning?"

So much for taking things slow and feeling her out. I suck at subtlety. That's Kerrington's specialty. I'm more like a bull with a red flag. I see it and go for it.

Nicole sinks into the water and doesn't answer me.

"Duchess," I warn. "We're here to help you, and that can't happen if we don't know what's going on."

She didn't get to this state overnight, or over a month or two. Our girl has been going through something for a while for her to be in this condition now.

"If you're not sick," I say cautiously, "then is it stress?"

"Why does it matter?"

"Because *you* matter," I'm quick to answer. "Always."

Jeez, it's getting hot in here. The steam in the bathroom feels like sticky fog in my lungs and my shirt is too tight.

"Why do I matter to you, Landon? What we…" She plays with the water a little bit and swallows hard. "What we did that night was just fun. It wasn't reality. It didn't matter."

She's a fool if she truly believes that.

Or maybe I'm the dumbass because I don't agree. One night with Nicole wasn't enough for me. It's put a huge rift in my relationship with Kerrington because I haven't told him what's up. I'm scared he'll leave me. But seeing how fast he was to swoop in like a knight in shining armor today and help her gives me hope that maybe he's a fool for her too.

Blowing out a long sigh, I sit on the floor and rest my chin on the edge of the tub like a puppy. "The night we shared you was the best night of my fucking life."

She freezes and looks straight ahead.

The growing silence is killing me.

"Why did you runaway, Nicole?" My heart gallops as I await her answer. "Answer me."

"Because," she whispers, "I was ashamed."

Her watery gaze swings to meet mine and all the air leaves my lungs. "Ashamed of what?"

It was a bad idea to ask that. She's likely ashamed of *me*. Sometimes I think Kerrington is too. Both of them are too good for me. I'm an embarrassment and a brat who doesn't give a shit about what others think of me.

"I..." Nicole bites her lip and shakes her head, swallowing whatever she was going to say.

"Did we do something wrong? Or me? Was it me? Did I—" Fucking hell, I thought I'd

Dommed her exactly like how she needed me to. I didn't think I'd gone overboard and everything we did that night was consensual. But maybe I'd misread something. "If I fucked things up, or scared you, I take full responsibility, and I'll make it up to you." It guts me to think I somehow messed this up. "You don't have to stay with us if you don't want. Kerrington can take you back to Mason's if you—"

"Landon," she all but growls. "Can I answer your question, or are you going to keep rambling?"

I shut up and stare at her.

God, I want to kiss her. Wrap her in my arms and hold her until she feels better. I want to feed her and bathe her and fuck her and worship her until whatever has gone wrong between us is fixed.

Nicole tucks her hair behind her ears, making her look adorable. "I was ashamed of myself."

"Why?"

She shakes her head. "Because I wasn't me that night."

I beg your finest pardon. She was *exactly* herself that night. She showed us the real Nicole that no one else has gotten to see. Talk about a motherfucking honor.

"Who were you then?" I ask cautiously.

"Duchess."

"Duchess." I repeat. "And I was Trick."

"Yes."

Is she trying to pretend that I'm not the same person? Yes, the honorific brings a level of escapism and fantasy to the scene, but I'm still me. I'm still Landon. The goofy, mindful, wild card with a big appetite motherfucker who had her choking on his cock. Twice.

"And when you woke up, you weren't Duchess anymore. You were Nicole."

"Correct."

"So, you ran."

"Yes."

Anger stirs in my chest. "Did you like Trick?"

"Yes," she says, a little softer. "And I like Landon too. I know you're the same person, but it just felt different. For me. Being called Duchess made me feel different."

Okay. I can work with that. "Did you like the way you felt, Duchess?"

Her eyes flutter as she looks up at me. "Yes."

Good. Because I'm going to make sure she feels that way again as soon as we understand what's going on with her body and stress levels.

My mind clicks back into Dom mode. "What do you need from me, Duchess?"

Her breath hitches, but she doesn't respond.

Okay. Let's try this another way. "Lift your arms out of the water and rest them on the sides of the tub for me."

She obeys with ease.

"Good girl." I grab a washcloth and soak it before running it down her neck and shoulders. "When Kerrington gets back, I want you to take three sips of water. Not four. Not two. *Three*. Do you understand?"

"Yes."

"Yes, what?"

"Yes, Trick."

My dick hardens immediately.

Kerrington walks in with perfect timing. I know he was listening on the other side of the door. He's carrying a tray with a glass of ice water and a small plate of chocolate mousse with one spoon. I grab the glass and hand it to her.

She gulps it greedily. Three times.

Next, I hold up a spoonful of the chocolate dessert. "Open."

Her jaw slackens and lips part.

"I want you to eat two bites of this for me, and then we're going to revisit those fries again." I push the spoon into her mouth and watch her lips wrap around the silverware.

"She takes orders so well," Kerrington says from behind me.

"Yeah, she does." My smile is so wide, I'm sure I look like a shark about to devour a little mermaid in my tub. "Take two more sips of water for us."

Nicole does it.

Jesus, it's like she's gone into some kind of trance. I can't tell if I like it or not. It's fun to give orders, but this is a little unsettling.

"Do you need us to take care of you like this, Nicole?" Kerrington asks gently. Dropping to his knees beside me at the tub, he brushes some of her hair away from her forehead. "There is no wrong answer, baby. As long as it's the truth."

Her cheeks turn red, eyes water. She doesn't answer.

"There's no judgement here," I reiterate. "And what happens in the hotel room, stays in the hotel room."

We never told Mason, Leah, or anyone else about our last threesome. We knew it could fuck up her home life and social circles if she was caught with us. Unfortunately, our time at the club was leaked, anyway. Christ, just dancing with her set off the rumor mills.

We took care of it swiftly, though.

If she needs to be a complete submissive to two Doms, we're more than happy to oblige. I get it. Sometimes you need to just stop thinking and be told what to do. Let the stress of life sit in the corner for a while and be controlled so you don't even have to come up with what to eat, or what chore to do next, or what to wear. Give all the burdens and responsibilities to someone you trust for a hot minute so you can fucking breathe.

"You have to use your words," Kerrington reminds her. "Nothing can happen here before then."

A tear slips down her cheek and my heart

cracks in half. Is it so hard to admit what you want?

"You can think about it," I casually say. "Take your time in here and relax. Finish drinking that water for us, too."

I tap Kerrington's shoulder, signaling him to get up, and we both leave her in the bathroom to consider our offer.

"I don't think she's going to go for it," Kerrington whispers. "We're not that lucky."

Luck has nothing to do with this. "She's desperate."

His brows pinch.

"She went to Mason's house," I explain. "You know she can't stand him. Their love-hate relationship has never changed. If anything, I suspect it got worse when he cut ties from everyone while she was left in hell after the gala. But she ran to *him*. And look at her. She's skin and bones."

Kerr nods with the corners of his mouth turned down. "Do you want her?"

"Yes," I admit without hesitation. The way he nearly flinches makes me pause. "Do you?"

He takes a moment, but finally says yes. His hesitation makes me reconsider our offer. "If this is going to fuck us up more, put more strain on what we have, then we need to stop before we start." His silence makes me tense. "Kerr. Are you listening to me?"

He grabs me by the throat and pushes me

back against the wall, holding my stare for so long, I melt. Then he kisses the ever-loving shit out of me. I have no clue what's gotten into him, but I love it. Crave it.

"It won't ruin us," he finally says after breaking away from me. Letting me go, he backs up, still catching his breath.

"But what if it does?" I'm scared for us. I want the three of us back together badly, but am I willing to risk everything for it? Fuck.

I am.

And I think Kerrington is too because he pops off with, "If it wrecks what you and I have, then maybe we were never meant to be."

My heart crashes.

He must see the devastation on my face because he adds, "Come on, Landon. Don't pretend you haven't been obsessing over her ever since she sprinted out of our bed the last time we did this." He closes in on me again. "I see you up in the middle of the night checking her socials. I know you think of her when you jerk off. And that bit about the special chocolates?" His gaze drags down my body. "How long have you been studying her? Memorizing every little thing about her?"

Since the day I first met her, but I can't say that. I don't think I could ever admit that.

"I'm just as observant as you are," I snap.

"It's not the same." Then his eyes round and brows pinch because it's dawned on him that it's *exactly* the same. "You're in love with her."

I shake my head, stupidly denying it. I can't lose Kerrington. I loved him first.

I want them both, but what if—

"Okay," Nicole says, walking out of the bathroom, wrapped in a towel. "My answer is yes."

"Yes, to what, exactly?" Kerrington takes the opportunity to escape our problem.

"Yes, I want to be treated like I was before with the two of you."

Kerrington stalks closer to her. "You'll submit wholly and completely?"

"Yes."

"And you'll stay in this room. No running away in the morning."

"No running away," she confirms.

"And you want us *both*?"

She first looks at him, then at me, and drops her head. "Yes."

"For how long?" Kerrington tilts her chin, so she'll look at him again. "How long do we get to have you, Duchess?"

"I… I'm not sure."

He lets her go and steps back, and I swear there's disappointment in his gaze. "We do nothing until you give us an end date."

Her hands ball into fists. "Goddamnit, Kerrington! I don't know. A week? A month?"

"Which is it?"

"A week," she huffs impatiently.

Kerrington looks towards me, his brow arched. "Do these conditions work for you, Landon?"

A week is nothing. It's not good enough. However, desperation urges me to take what I can fucking get. "Yes."

"Good." Kerrington points at the sofa and says to Nicole, "Go over there and sit down, Duchess."

She gracefully and quietly, walks over to the couch and sits.

"Eat the rest of the French fries in that bag," I say, my pulse racing.

Nicole snatches the bag and grabs a handful, stuffing them in her mouth.

"Slowly," Kerrington growls. "We don't want you to choke or make yourself sick, baby."

She swallows and tries again, only putting two fries in her pretty mouth this time.

"Good girl." I fall to my knees at her feet. "Do you remember your safe word?"

"Teapot."

"Perfect." Kerrington sits next to her, and we make sure she finishes her meal. "How do you feel now?"

"Full." She leans back, sighing, and rests her head against his shoulder.

"Not full enough," I tease, tugging her towel away to expose her body. "Sit in Kerrington's lap."

He lifts Nicole easily and settles her on top

of him. "Spread your legs, Duchess. Trick has gone too long without eating too."

He hasn't called me Trick since that night the three of us shared. Hearing him use the name now stirs up a lot of things inside of me. We stare at each other for several heartbeats, and then I devour the woman between us.

Chapter 7

Nicole

Threading my fingers through Landon's thick, wavy blond hair, I ride his face a little harder. The man's mouth is incredibly skilled, and it will not take me long to reach a climax. I've been positively touch starved.

"That's it, baby. Take what you need from him." Kerrington's hands remain latched on my thighs, keeping me spread. I feel dirty and exquisite at the same time.

Pressing back into Kerrington's chest, I tip my head and squeeze my eyes shut, riding that glorious climb to the peak of ecstasy. Landon shoves two fingers inside me, hooking them to hit my g-spot and I finally unravel.

"There she goes," Kerrington coos in this calming, satisfied tone. "That's our good girl. Come all over Landon's mouth. Soak him, sweetheart."

And I do. My thighs shake and body practically convulses with the roaring orgasm I have. It's been a long time since I've come like this. Two guesses when that time was, and the first guess doesn't count.

Kerrington's erection rubs against my ass while I sit on his lap. There's lust in Landon's gaze when he looks at me and drags his tongue along my pussy. The heat between these two makes me dissolve into a puddle of neediness.

"Fuck, I've missed your taste, Duchess." Landon climbs up my body until his mouth is inches from mine. Mischief paints a smile on his handsome face. "Taste her, Kerr."

I lean a little to the left, making it easier for them to kiss. God, I love the groans they both make when their mouths meet.

"Tastes like Heaven, doesn't she?" Landon asks in this deep, sexy tone.

"Fuck yeah she does." Kerrington grabs him by the back of the neck and kisses him again, this time deeper, and my hand slips between my legs to rub out another orgasm. Only one of them stops me before I can see my mission through.

"No touching yourself, Duchess." Kerrington pulls me back until I'm flush against him again. "If you want to come, ask us for permission. Understand?"

"Yes."

Something tight in my chest eases a little more. Every time I take orders from one of these guys, I get a little more relaxed. It's easy. Nice. "I want to come again… please."

"Mmm, she uses such good manners." Landon runs his hands over my body, waking it up, and my blood catches fire. I'm hot all over.

Kerrington joins the touching party and whispers in my ear, "My turn." He picks me up and turns me over on the couch. "Face the wall." He lightly taps my ass as I get on my knees. "Bend over as far as you can."

Draping myself off the back of the sofa, I feel lightheaded with need.

"Goddamn, look at her." He slaps my ass again, this time a little harder, and my pussy clenches. "She's glistening from that O you gave her, Trick."

I look over my shoulder at Landon, who's now sitting in a chair opposite us. He's pulling his dick out to stroke it. "I want her wetter for us."

Kerrington chuckles as he runs his hands over my ass cheeks, and I brace for whatever he might do to me. He's an ass man, through and through, and the only one I've let go into my backdoor. Will he do that now?

"I'm going to lick you, finger you, and rim you," he warns. "And when you're about to come, I'm going to deny you and have you begging for it."

Oh. My. God.

"You okay with that, Duchess?"

I nod enthusiastically.

"Use your words," Landon orders. "Or you get nothing, and you'll be staying in that position for an hour as punishment."

"Yes!" I shout. "Yes, yes."

Kerrington kneels on the couch behind me and presses his groin to my bare ass. "That's our good girl."

He peppers hot kisses down my spine and nips both butt cheeks. Then he spreads them obscenely and drags his tongue along my pussy, tasting me. "Better than champagne." He plunges a finger inside me and pulls it out, sucking it clean. "You're an addictive little thing, aren't you, Duchess?"

I don't know how to respond to that.

He smacks my ass. "Answer me."

"I'm sorry."

He runs his hands over my butt again. "Sorry for what?"

"Being addictive."

"And why would that be something to apologize for?" He spanks me again, but it's not hard.

"Because… addictions are problems. They're bad."

"Are you bad?" He spanks me again before licking my asshole, rimming it with his tongue while he fingers my pussy a little more.

"Maybe," I whisper with a half groan. Holy shit that feels amazing.

"Maybe we like bad." He runs his tongue along my tight muscle again, making my toes curl. "Maybe we've missed bad."

I hold my breath, concentrating on my body instead of his words because I'm scared of the emotions that have awakened.

When he shoves two fingers into my pussy, and another in my ass, I freeze completely. His speed alternates between fast and slow and lightning speed. He brings me to the edge over and over until I'm sweating and so tense I could snap.

"Neither of you can come until I tell you differently," he barks.

Landon groans. I suck in a harsh breath and hold it.

"Now *beg*, Duchess." Kerrington's fingers are pure torture inside me. It's the best worst thing I've ever felt.

I love it.

"Please." I suck in another harsh breath. "Please let me come. I need to."

He picks up speed. "Beg harder."

"Please!" My thighs shake and fingers dig into the back of the sofa. "Please, I have to come. I… I can't hold it anymore."

Landon groans louder, and I can hear him jerking off. The sound of him pleasuring himself has me reeling. I look over my shoulder so I can watch, but Kerrington blocks my view. "Turn around, Duchess. You have to earn the right to watch him."

I'm going to be sick. Nausea swirls in my belly and stars dance in my vision. "Goddamnit, Kerrington, let me come. *Now!*"

His speed shifts to a slower one, and I nearly

explode with frustration.

"You've missed us, haven't you?"

"I'm not feeding your ego," I grit out. "Let me come."

Landon groans again, louder. "Kerr, I'm too close."

"Stop touching yourself then."

Landon lets out a guttural noise and his breaths saw out of him, but I think he's just obeyed Kerrington.

"That's a good boy." Kerr runs his hand down my spine, bringing his attention effortlessly back to me. "How bad do you want to watch him explode, baby?"

"So bad."

"Squeeze my fingers for a count of five."

"What?"

"You heard me," he growls, spanking my ass once more.

I try to focus on controlling my body and work my Kegel exercises to grip his fingers while they're inside me.

"Five, four, three, two… one." Kerrington twists his hand a little, working my ass and pussy more. "That's a good girl. Trick, bring your chair over here and sit in front of her."

Landon drags the oversized lounger across the living room and parks it where he's told. The man looks as wound up as I am, and I had no idea he'd gotten naked. So, when he sits down and licks his lips, I'm momentarily stunned by his beauty.

Landon's built like a Greek god.

"Stroke yourself at my speed," Kerrington orders. Then he pumps his fingers into my holes again while Landon keeps the same pace and jerks himself. "Who should come first, you or her?"

"Her," Landon growls. "Always her."

Kerrington plays with my body like it's his favorite toy. "Beg, baby."

"Please… oh god, Kerrington, please give me this. I need it."

He fucks me harder with his hand. My entire body seems to coil and heat. "I'm so close."

"I know you are." He spanks my ass with his free hand and says to Landon, "Watch our girl come undone."

He slams into me, finger fucking me hard and fast until I explode. Screaming with all my might, I fly apart. My vision bursts white and when it's over, I collapse, gasping for air, sobbing.

"Shh." Kerrington's on me in a blink, smoothing back my hair and kissing my neck. "It's not over yet, baby. I've got you." He rubs my clit in slow circles, and I have no idea how I can possibly come anymore. But heat blooms inside me again and I move my hips to ride his hand. Kerrington smothers me with his scent and touch, his body presses hard against mine. He cups my chin, angling it, so I'm staring straight at Landon. Kerrington's voice shoots lightning through my body when he says, "Come for us, Trick."

We both watch in awe as Landon strokes himself a few more times and ejaculates all over his stomach and thighs. I can see his dick jerk, pulsing, throbbing as his orgasm runs through him. His head's tipped back. His chest expands and contracts with each deep breath he musters.

Fucking hell, he's stunning.

"Your turn again," Kerrington whispers in my ear. He rubs my clit harder, faster, and bites down on my neck.

I come on his hand while Landon stares at me with a hooded gaze.

We're both panting by the time we're done, and I think my body is melting into the furniture.

"You did such a good job," he says. "Both of you."

Landon stands with this lazy, satisfied smile on his face, and approaches the back of the couch. They kiss, with me sandwiched between them again, and I'm suddenly hungry for more. Reaching out, I grab Landon's dick, which is still wet and sticky from his orgasm, and suck it into my mouth.

"Fuuuuuck," he whispers.

His deflating cock is soft between my lips and easy to play with. I roll my tongue over the tip and suck on it like a pacifier. Shame heats my face, but I can't seem to stop. This feels too good. It's calming.

Kerrington peppers more kisses on my back

and works his way up to my shoulders. Gathering my hair in his hand, he pulls gently, making my head tip back. "That's enough for today, baby. Let him go."

I stop sucking and Landon steps away, letting his dick plop out of my mouth. I miss his taste already. "But I'm not done."

"Neither are we," Landon promises. "Now get dressed."

"Why?"

He tips my chin, smiling down at me. "Just do what you're told, Duchess. Follow the rules like a good girl so we can keep rewarding you."

When Kerrington helps me off the couch, my legs are wobbly and laughter bubbles out of me. I honestly can't remember the last time I felt this good. "I think you guys broke me."

"Not yet," Kerr warns. "But if you want us to, we will."

Chapter 8

Kerrington

I'm in deep trouble.

I wasn't kidding when I said Nicole was addictive. She's going to be a fucking problem if I can't rein in my goddamn urges and get some control over myself.

Just now, I wanted nothing more than to fuck her senseless and make Landon watch. Make him shake with need. Have him begging on his knees for me to do the same thing to his ass as I wanted to do to hers.

And watching her suck on him like she has some kind of oral fixation and his cock in her mouth brought her soothing comfort?

Damn. I want to experience it myself.

Except we haven't worked out the dynamics of our throuple yet and I'm Landon's Dom. His needs are my priority. And her needs, it seems, are *his* priority.

When we've taken a woman to our bed before, we played around and had fun, but Landon remained a sub the whole time. Always.

With Nicole, he's completely different. I like seeing him this way. He's an excellent switch. But what happens when this week is over? Are we just supposed to go back to being the way we were before, or will there be a Nicole-shaped hole in our relationship that will eventually break us apart for good?

"Smoke's coming out of your ears." Landon's dressed from the waist down. He snags his shirt off the floor and saunters over to me with a playful smile on his lips. When he sees my face, however, his humor fades. "Kerr, what's wrong?"

"Nothing."

He drops into serious mode on me. "If you don't want to do this, we'll stop. We can bring her back to Mason's and step back. She didn't come to us to begin with. We practically kidnapped her."

He's right, but the thought of giving Nicole back feels even worse than keeping her here with us. "We need to understand what's wrong with her."

"We will." Landon's brow pinches, and he squeezes my shoulders. "But I'm still yours, Kerr. With or without Nicole."

My heart clenches and I can't get my brain and mouth to sync up. Staring into his eyes, I want to confess a lot of shit I've been holding back, but now isn't the time. So, I distract us both by kissing him. I can still smell Nicole's arousal on his lips. My cock stirs and I deepen our connection by grabbing the back of his head and kiss him harder.

He groans in my mouth, and I swallow it. His hands skate up my sides until one hand grips the back of my neck, the other is buried in my hair, and he yanks me by the roots. I hiss in half pain, half pleasure. "Watch it, *brat*."

"You're so turned on right now you can't think straight," he says with a shit-eating grin. "I don't think I've ever seen you this way before."

I want to tell him he's wrong, but I grab his hard dick instead. "Pot meet kettle."

"Fuck right, I'm turned on."

We're playing a dangerous game, and I don't want any of us to get hurt.

"You have to be careful," I warn. "Her aftercare is just as important as everything else. And her mental state right now is… unstable."

"I know." He lets out a heavy sigh.

We're both worried about Nicole and giving her physical attention is only part of what she needs.

Landon cringes. "Does it make me a real asshole to be a little relieved that she's hit rock bottom, though?"

His tone has my heart deflating.

"I want her happy and taken care of," he explains. "It should be us that gets that privilege. No one else. And…" He rubs the back of his neck and winces. "Fucking hell, Kerr. If she had to sink to the bottom to be with us again, I'm—"

"I'm ready," Nicole announces from our bedroom door. She's in one of my button-down shirts and has a thin belt wrapped around her waist to make it look more like a short dress.

Oh hell no. "It's too cold outside to wear that."

"You'll keep me warm." Nicole shoots back just before glancing over at Landon, seeking his approval too.

"Fucking. Stunning." He prowls over and kisses her with all the finesse of a charming prince.

Her laugh spreads heat through my cold chest. I completely understand Landon's confession and I think that makes us both grade-A assholes because having her with us is all I've wanted. If we're her rock bottom, so be it. I don't care what we are to her as long as we're *something*.

"So…" She nervously tucks her hair behind her ear. "Where are we going, boys?"

"Yeah, Landon. Where are we going?" I cock my brow and wait for him to speak.

"I have no idea." Landon grabs her hand and kisses the back of it. "But we're going to look good doing it."

Typical Landon. He always thinks he can sail through life with no compass or instruction. I'm the opposite. I have a well-thought-out plan for everything, including this trip. Aaaand then Nicole happened, knocking everything off its axis, even if I'm secretly happy she's back in our arms. I guess not everything can have an itinerary.

"Kerrington, where do you want to go?" Nicole asks.

Honestly? Nowhere. I'm tired, not hungry, and I'm still locked on the fear of what will become of us after this week is over. Nicole obviously gives Landon something I can't, and she fills a hole in my heart that Landon can't touch.

Jesus… are Landon and I really not enough for each other? Has that been our un-climbable wall this whole time?

Is Nicole the missing piece or a motherfucking wrecking ball?

I'm not good at relationships or expressing feelings, and I never saw this dynamic with Nicole coming. I've been content with Landon for two years, and when we get an itch, we bring a woman in and scratch it. Temporarily.

Nicole's not temporary material. She's eternity. Strong and broken. Funny and terrifying. Beautiful and lethal. Because mark my words, if we aren't careful, her leaving us again will probably kill my relationship with Landon.

I think I'm going to be sick.

"Earth to Kerrington," Landon says. Concern dances across his face when I swing my gaze towards him.

My chest is too tight. I can't take a full breath.

"Kerr," he says with worry. "Hey, whoa."

Next thing I know, my ass is planted in a chair and Landon's squatting down in front of me. I don't like looking weak in front of him. I don't like feeling all these fucked up emotions.

Landon glares at me. The conversation we just tabled hits me like a sledgehammer.

Landon's right to be worried about us.

I'm just as fucking terrified.

I can't lose you. Ever. The words catch in my throat as I stare at him.

He shakes his head, as if hearing what I can't say. "We're solid."

"Are we?"

"Absolutely."

The pain in my chest doesn't ease. I think it's because I have something more to confess and now would be a great time to say it, except my mouth and brain keep misfiring. Especially when I notice Nicole watching us with a deep wrinkle between her perfectly shaped eyebrows.

I don't ever want her to think her presence is a problem. She needs us right now, and we need her too. At least I know I fucking do.

A shaky exhale leaves me. "We have to always be honest with each other."

"And we have been," Landon says, then tips his head at me suspiciously. "Haven't we?"

Loaded. Fucking. Question.

Say it, Kerrington. Just fucking say the words!

Again, my mouth runs dry, and I remain

silent, staring at Landon until movement catches my attention. Nicole works her way towards the bedroom door, and I snap into action. There's no way I'm going to let her walk out of this motherfucking suite without us and I know damn well she's going for her bag so she can run again. "Don't you dare move, Duchess."

She freezes.

Turning my attention back to Landon, I answer his honesty question. "Yes."

The lie cuts me in half, but I can't admit the whole truth right now. I'm still trying to figure things out for myself.

"Shopping," Landon suddenly says. Standing up, he puts on his shirt and grabs his boots.

"We're going to get a little retail therapy tonight and then we're coming home, piling into the king-sized bed, and vibing."

Nicole and I look at each other, and I think she's waiting for me to approve.

"Okay," I say calmly, rising to my feet. "Let's go."

Grabbing Nicole's hand, I give it a reassuring squeeze and we leave the penthouse, with Landon leading the way.

Chapter 9

Landon

Something's up with Kerrington. I can tell he's holding something back and I want to know what it is. My attempt at reassuring him we're solid in our relationship did nothing to cut the fear radiating from him. So, I'm going to take this night in a more fun direction instead.

Look, I don't mean to be a fucknut, and I definitely do *not* want Nicole miserable, but I am thrilled she's with us. A week isn't long, but it'll give us time to convince her she should be with us permanently. I'd love nothing more than to wake up with both of them every goddamn morning.

Does that make me a selfish prick? I don't care. I want that life. I'll do anything to make it happen too. My feelings for Nicole are deeper than a fun fuck. She brings out a side of me I rarely get to indulge in. With Kerrington, I'm a bratty sub, but I ache to have someone I can dominate, and that will never be him. He's perfect as is.

We're the opposites attract trope to the max.

Kerr's a broody, strict control freak. I'm wild with no fucks to give about anything other than having a good time, being there for my friends, and making as much money as possible.

My life goal is to own an island one day.

Tonight, however, my only priority is to make Nicole feel safe and give her whatever she needs to heal. I've known Nicole for almost as long as I've been best friends with Mason, Kerrington, and Gage. At first, she put me off because she was such a raging bitch, but it didn't take long to see it was an act.

She pretends to hate Mason, but deep down, she values his friendship more than anything. I think the reason they were so volatile over the years was because of the arranged marriage thing. Thank God Mason took care of that before it turned into a nightmare for them both.

And I've always noticed the way Kerrington stares at her. We've never discussed it, but he has big feelings for her. I can tell. I just wish he'd say what's in his heart, so I know my place in it.

"You hungry?" Kerrington asks Nicole from the back seat. She's up front with me this time, making me feel all kinds of special.

"Not really. No."

"You need to eat more, Duchess. We'll pick up some pizzas on the way back and order room service." I place my hand on her thigh. She's cold to the touch, so I turn the heat on in the car for her. She should have put on leggings under the shirt dress. Kerrington's right, it's too cold for her chosen outfit. I should have told her what to wear. *Fuck.* I'm botching my role already. Guess I'm a little rusty. Cranking the heat to the max, I aim the vents in her direction.

"I think I'd like to set some boundaries," she says, staring out the window.

I glance at Kerrington in my rearview mirror, and we both nod. "Absolutely."

Nicole clears her throat, and I swear she goes into business mode on us with how her tone and posture change. "I don't want to think. I don't want to decide. I don't want to work. I need to check out and just..." Her voice fades and she crosses her arms, hugging herself.

"And just what, Duchess?" Kerrington presses.

She shrugs and leans her head against the window, going radio silent on us.

"Be our toy?" The question flies out of my mouth before I can filter it. Jesus, I'm an asshole for saying that.

"Yes," she whispers.

Ex-squeeze me? Did she just say *yes* to that?

Kerrington and I look at each other in the mirror again, and the shock on his face almost makes me laugh.

"You want to be our fucktoy, Nicole?" He leans forward and cups her chin, forcing her to make eye contact with him.

I almost rear-end the person in front of me

because I'm too caught up in their connection and not paying enough attention to the road. "Shit! Sorry."

"Answer me, Duchess." Kerrington keeps his focus on her while mine is on the traffic light.

Calling her Duchess must trigger the response that Nicole wouldn't otherwise give. "Yes."

My stomach drops and leaps at the same time, which makes me dizzy. Having a bombshell like Nicole be our fucktoy is a goddamn wet dream come true. But I don't want her used like that all the time. She's not a flesh light, she's the woman I lo—

Like a whole lot.

Yup, I like her. Have for a while. Like is the word, right? That means you think about them all the time, light up on the inside when you see them, worry for them, crave them, are in awe of them, can't stop looking at them, stalk them on social media and get all butt hurt when they ghost you after the most passionate night of your life.

What I feel for Kerrington is different.

He's home to me. We're not perfect, but it doesn't matter because to me, what we have is better than perfect. I've never told him that, though. I don't think he's ready to hear my confession, just like Nicole wasn't ready to hear how I felt that night six months ago when I finally got her in our bed.

"—out for a few days. Then things can go

back to normal."

Shit, my thoughts got too loud, and I missed what she said. "Say that again, please?"

"I said I want to check out for a few days. Then things can go back to normal."

"Why does it feel like we're the toys in this situation?" Kerrington asks with a twinge of humor.

"I suppose maybe you are." Nicole's smile cracks across her face and I suddenly don't care who's playing with who.

"Define going back to normal," Kerrington says cautiously.

"I'll go back to New York and you guys can go back to California."

I feel sick again. Does she think we can walk away from her so easily? I know she certainly doesn't have a problem running from us, but damn, this hurts.

"Bold of you to assume you're going to get away from us again, Duchess." Kerrington leans back and smirks. "If we have to, we'll put a short leash on your sweet ass. Ghosting us again is not an option."

My throat tightens. "He's right. If you want to do this, you can't run again when you're forced to face us in the morning."

"I'm already agreeing to be with you for a week. That's commitment enough."

I pull into a parking lot and cut the engine. "Not for me."

The look on her face is half fear, half I don't even know what. Relief maybe?

"You're right." I clear my throat. "We need boundaries before we do anything else."

Because I have a horrible feeling all three of us will get hurt if we aren't careful and I'll do anything to protect the ones I love.

Chapter 10

What do they want from me? I'm already feeling too much pressure from everyone else in my life and that's the reason I left New York and ran to Mason and Leah's. Isn't it enough to offer them sex, however they want it, whenever they want it, just so I can get out of my head for a while?

Needy motherfuckers.

And yet, when I see the anxiousness in Landon's gaze, and the trepidation in Kerrington's, I'm suddenly reminded that they're not toys at all. They're humans with genuine feelings and I think running from their hotel last time hurt them.

I never want to cause them pain.

Mason and I have been frenemies since childhood, but Landon and Kerrington are my friends. I always look forward to seeing them again, even when I pretend I can't stand to be around them.

It's a coping mechanism. One I've tried to

grow out of but can't.

Being a tough, callous bitch is the reason I'm so good at my job. And being so good at my job is the reason I'm falling apart. I can't keep going like this.

That night of the gala was a turning point for me. I got a taste of a different life. A different Nicole. And I want her back.

"It's not a coincidence that I showed up at Mason's," I admit. "Grace told me you were going to be there visiting this week so I…" Jesus, I can't even finish my sentence. Why did I just blurt that out? I'm an idiot. I'm suddenly way too hot and I don't feel good. "I need air. It's stifling in here." I turn my frustration to the vents and smack them all closed.

Grace is the only one who knows that I've fallen for two men. *These* two men. When she found out they were coming to Mason's, she didn't hesitate to call and tell me, urging me to come here and figure my shit out.

"Jesus fucking Christ." Landon climbs out of the car, storms over to my side, and rips the door open.

"What are you doing?" I ask as he unbuckles my seatbelt and practically hauls me out of the car.

"What I want." Landon crushes his mouth to mine and for a moment, I'm free-falling. It's fucking spectacular.

Landon has this phenomenal magnetism to

him. He's warm sunshine and joy. He's a day at the beach after a decade of living in a cold cave. He kisses with so much passion and hunger that I can't help but be swept away by it.

When he deepens our kiss, I'm pressed against the back door and my outfit is showing too much leg and ass. The idea of Kerrington watching us from the backseat makes me giddy.

I guide Landon's hand between my legs, giving him permission to do more than just kiss me. This feels naughty and exciting and completely out of my realm of acceptable ways to behave.

I love it.

"Bad girl," he growls with a smile. "You're gonna have Kerrington feeling all left out."

"He'll get his turn, eventually." My breaths punch out of me because I'm too riled up and excited. We're in broad daylight, in a public parking lot, and—

"Oh god," I moan when he shoves a finger inside my pussy.

Landon kisses and nips my neck while he fingers me. I hook one leg around his waist and cling to his shoulders for balance. It's cold out, and white puffs of air form from my breath, but I'm burning up.

"Our Duchess is so fucking wet."

Well, that's what happens when you're basically being ravaged by the human version of Apollo. The fact that there's an entire world around us, and we could get caught, amplifies this moment and makes me wetter.

"Goddamn, listen to your cunt." Landon moves his finger faster inside me. "You enjoy being watched, don't you?"

"Yes, I… guess… I do." Fucking Hell, I'm close to exploding. "I like that… Kerr is… fuuuuuck, Landon you feel so good."

He bites down on my neck and pumps his finger faster, harder, hooking it to hit something inside me that makes my toes curl. I come around his hand, my nails digging into his shoulders while I ride the wave. It's pure, head spinning ecstasy.

"That's our good girl." Landon kisses me softly and pulls back to give me breathing space. I tug my outfit back down and stumble forward a little, giggling. That was a lot of fun.

Kerrington finally opens the car door and unfolds from the backseat. He looks all worked up but keeps his cool. Landon smirks at him. "Want a taste?"

Without saying a word, Kerrington snatches Landon's wrist and sucks his finger with my orgasm all over it.

I'd give my left tit to see them kiss right now.

"Wearing your shirt, and being so aroused, she smells like you and her combined," Landon says quietly. "That's a heady fucking combo."

Kerrington smiles as he looks over at me,

holding his hand out for me to take. I lace my fingers with his and we walk like we didn't just have a scene in the middle of the parking lot.

"Where are we?"

"You'll see." Landon grabs my other hand, and I have a moment where I instinctively want to pull away from them both. People are going to think we're a throuple. They'll judge.

Sex in public aside, this feels more taboo. More real. More vulnerable.

But the look of pure joy on Landon's face stops me from letting go. I wish I was more like him. He genuinely lives life exactly how he wants and if someone else doesn't like it, that's their problem, not his. I want to give no fucks about what everyone else thinks of me, just like he does. So, I squeeze his hand harder and then do the same with Kerrington. They both return the favor, which brings me relief.

Until Kerrington lets go and puts his hands in his pockets.

Why does that feel like a rejection?

He's always been like that. Whenever I catch him glancing at me, he looks away with this annoyed expression on his ridiculously handsome face. I can't tell if it's an act or not. But when he touches me… kisses me… fucks me… I swear I'm his entire universe. That's how he makes me feel. I'm not just special, and I'm not just a good time. I'm his *everything*.

Talk about being delulu.

Wow. I need therapy.

"After you," Landon says, opening the door to the shop.

Holy mother of dildos.

"We're retail therapy shopping in a *sex toy store*?" I whisper-yell.

"This is the boundary conversation center."

Kerrington is already heading over to the cock rings.

Oh my god, I can't believe they brought me here. I wouldn't be caught dead in a store like this back at home. "And how are we discussing boundaries here, *Trick*?"

He comes up behind me and wraps his arms around my middle, rocking me side to side. "Peruse and bring us five things you want to use. Also point out products that are a hard limit for you. And if you don't know if you're into something or not, put it on the counter and we'll discuss."

I can't just openly shop like that. I feel too seen. "I'm not sure I'm comfortable with this," I admit.

"The toys or the store?"

"Shopping for this stuff in public."

"Okay." He hooks his arm with mine. "No buying from here then. We can look in person and buy online. No biggie."

Some of the tightness in my chest eases.

"What did you find, Kerr?" Landon steers us towards the back, where Kerrington is now studying a wall of whips and crops.

"Duchess, do you like being spanked?"

I gawk at Kerrington. He knows the answer. He's spanked me before. But the way he's patiently waiting for me to use my words has me opening my fat mouth. "Umm. Yes. I mean, I liked it when you bent me over your lap and used your hand last time."

Kerrington's smile goes a mile wide, making him look devastatingly handsome. He's already got the broody, dark haired, sex in a suit thing going on. That genuine smile makes him look like a very good, bad idea.

He plucks a flogger off the wall that has soft fabric roses on the tips.

"We're going to buy online instead," Landon whispers discreetly.

Kerrington nods in understanding and goes to hang the flogger back up on the wall when I stop him.

"No, buy it now. We're already here." I don't think I can wait for shipping, even if it's next day. Courage takes hold of me, and I glance around, eager to try new things. "We're going to need a basket or a shopping cart."

Landon chuckles. "I don't think they have carts here. It's not a grocery store."

Well, now I feel dumb. I've never been to a sex shop before. The one vibrator I have I bought online. Crossing my arms, I look down at my feet and try to swallow the embarrassment.

Kerrington uses the handle of the flogger to lift my chin up. "Don't worry. We've got big arms. We can carry whatever you want us to buy, Duchess."

A shopping spree in a sex shop?

Never have I ever.

"Check these out." Landon goes over to a selection of collars. He playfully runs his hand over a metal link leash.

Okay. I'm doing this. I'm going to break down another one of my walls and find some sexual freedom. When Kerrington threatened to put me on a short leash earlier, I'd be a liar to say the idea didn't turn me on.

"This one," I say, pointing at a pink leather collar with a dark metal chain. "I want this one."

Landon cocks an eyebrow at me as if asking *Are you sure*?

I roll my shoulders back and hold my ground. "Are you carrying it, or will I have to do it myself?"

He plucks it off the wall and closes the space between us. "Maybe you should try it on first, to make sure it feels comfortable."

My heart hammers when he wraps the leather around my throat and buckles it.

"Jesus," Kerrington murmurs.

My cheeks heat as they both eat me alive with their gazes.

Landon licks his lips. "Goddamn, I'm so fucking hard right now."

"Feel him," I blurt in a quiet voice.

Kerrington's brow furrows. "Excuse me?"

"Feel how hard he is." I nervously play with the leash attached to my collar. "I want to watch you touch him."

Kerr swallows hard. Landon's face falls into a mask. I think I've somehow stepped out of line. "What?"

Surely, they're not shy with each other. Besides, we just had a fingering session in broad daylight just a few minutes ago and they didn't mind that. This is no different.

"Hmph." Landon playfully pushes Kerrington back. "He has to earn the right to get to my dick."

Funny. Six months ago, we didn't have to earn anything because we eagerly gave each other anything we wanted. I've lost count of how many fantasies I've had about it since.

Kerrington stalks forward, making Landon back up until his ass hits the display of vibrators on a table. "I don't have to earn it," Kerr growls. "I *own* it." His hand drops between Landon's thighs, and he grabs the bulge there.

Thank God we're the only ones in the store right now, because the noise that comes out of me is pure porn audio gold. I quickly clamp my hands over my mouth to shut myself up. Eyes blowing wide with embarrassment, I look away from them.

It's way too easy to forget myself around

these two.

The tension between them has always been like this. I swear they build it up on purpose.

Growling, Kerrington backs away from Landon and casually heads over to the game table next.

I run my nails down Landon's back. He's tense. Warm. Does that mean he's turned on or uncomfortable? I don't know him well enough to figure it out yet. "Are you okay?"

His blue eyes lock with mine. "Never better."

It sounds like a lie. Looks like one too.

Before I can ask what's going through his head, Landon clears his throat. "Pick one of these, Duchess."

"That one," I say, not really paying attention.

Grabbing what looks like a clit stimulator, he plays with the settings. "Nice. And what about those?"

I join him at the display of rabbits and wands. "The teal one is cute."

"*Cute?*" He picks it up. "Cute will be seeing you orgasm so hard your cum drips down this thing."

My thighs clench with need. "Only if you're lucky."

He snatches a boxed one from the table and then points at the butt plugs. "How about a remote controlled one?"

"I'm not sure I'm ready for that."

Landon arches his brow. "What about for me?"

My gaze drifts to Kerrington, who I know damn well is listening, even if it looks like he isn't. Does he use one of these with Landon often? Fuck, I'd love to see that.

Landon runs the back of his hand softly across my collarbone, teasing the tops of my breasts with the lightest touch. "Do you want to watch Kerrington make me come with one of these, Duchess?"

More than anything. "Yes."

Landon grabs a silver one from the table and winks. "He's ruthless when he wants to be."

"Only when you're asking for it," Kerrington says, proving my theory that he was eavesdropping.

I'm completely enraptured by these two, and I want to keep the buildup going. "What about those?" Heading over to the wall of bondage products, I pluck a package of nipple rings and toss them to Kerrington.

Then I snag a spreader bar and give it to Landon, who says, "Fuck yes. Now we're talking."

My excitement escalates. "The bench too?"

Kerr nods. "I'll have the employee grab it. Keep going, Duchess. You're doing so good."

Happiness seeps into my system, and I bite my lip to keep from smiling too big. "Umm, what about a cock cage?"

Landon drops two of our boxes and fumbles to pick them up. Kerrington grins. It's pure mayhem. "Yeah."

"Yeah?" Landon snaps.

"*Yeah*." Kerrington tips his head. "Unless you don't want it. Is that a hard limit, all of a sudden?"

Landon's cheeks mottle red. "No."

"Good boy. Duchess, grab him the blue one."

"It'll match his eyes," I say, practically giddy.

"Speaking of…" Kerrington looks around the store. "Where are the blindfolds?"

"Up front," Landon answers. "Grab two."

The leash dangling from my neck rattles as I rush to the front of the store and snag two black silk blindfolds from their hooks. Oh, handcuffs! I grab two of them as well.

"This is fun!" A giggle escapes me as I get a few more interesting looking things and carry my goodies back to them. "What next?"

"Lube," Kerr answers with a panty-melting smile. "Lots and lots of lube."

Chapter 11

Kerrington

By the time we get back from shopping, Nicole's attitude has changed six times, and I can't figure her out at all. One minute she's happy, the next she's closed up. I don't like it and haven't forgotten the fact that earlier she mentioned she knew we'd be at Mason's this week and that's why she came.

If she wanted to see us so badly, why not show up at our door instead? Hell, even a phone call would have been nice.

While I carry in the bench, Landon takes care of the rest of our bags, and we dump everything onto the living room floor.

Nicole doesn't touch a thing. She just saunters into the suite and looks around like she's unsure what to do next.

"Go take a shower, Duchess." I slap her ass, sending her to the bathroom. "We'll take care of all this and order dinner."

"Umm. Okay."

Once she disappears into our bedroom, I

turn my attention to Landon. "We need to figure out our—"

Landon's on me in a blink, crushing his mouth to mine, and marching me backwards until I hit the wall. The fire in his eyes spreads through my chest and straight to my dick.

The tension we toyed with in the store roars back to life and we volley dominance like he has any chance of gaining it over me. I love it.

"Easy, Trick." I wrap my hand around his throat and hold him captive. I slide my free hand down his chest and grab his hard cock, rubbing my palm against it. "So fucking sensitive."

"Give me something," he begs.

"What is it you want?" I'd give this man everything if I thought myself capable of it.

"Anything."

He always says this shit to me, but it hits differently this time.

Cupping the side of his face, I hold him steady and stare at him. Does he know how much he means to me? Does he know I'd burn the world down for him?

Does he know I'm also in love with Nicole and therefore can't figure out what I want?

"Define *anything*," I nip his earlobe.

Landon's knees almost buckle, and he groans in the most delicious way. Then he grabs the nape of my neck and holds me still. "I want the truth. I want to know what you're hiding, Kerrington."

Fuuuuck.

I can't give him that. I can't admit that Nicole seared her name on my soul a long time ago. I can't say that I'd count down the days for her next college visit, and once we all graduated and went our merry ways, I always looked forward to those pretentious galas we'd attend together. I never cared what the money raised was for. I just wanted to see Nicole again and if that meant buying a ten-thousand-dollar plate of shitty food to do it, so be it. Money well spent.

On the outside, I'm calculating and quiet. But I'm also clueless on how to show my love. Behind closed doors, however, I become someone else. Someone who takes charge and wants to spoil the hell out of those I'd die for.

Sex with Landon isn't just about playing with our kinky sides. It's the only time I don't worry about anything and can give him all the attention he deserves. He's the reason I wake up every day and try to be a better man.

"I love you," I say gruffly, still holding his face. "Never think otherwise."

This is the first time I've said those words out loud, even though I've said them in my head, and with my body, a million times before now.

It's the only truth I'm willing to give him.

Landon swallows hard, his mouth clamped tightly shut. I swear the blood drains from his face. That truth bomb was definitely *not* something he was prepared to hear.

Great. Now I feel like a fool.

"It's okay. You don't have to say it back." I honestly think I'm only confessing it now because if we survive this experience with Nicole, it'll be a miracle. And I don't believe in miracles. If I can tell him how I feel, deep down in my soul, at least once, then he'll know what he means to me when this gets messy and blows up in our faces.

Landon's mouth parts as if he's about to say something, but I kiss him instead. I don't want him feeling obligated to respond, and I think we're all confused right now. His mouth is soft and full against mine. He smells incredible. Running my hand up the back of his head, I grab a handful of his hair and tug it. He groans against me and pulls back.

Our gazes lock, and there's a lot of heat between us again.

Being with Landon is the easiest thing in the world. Loving him is next level, and I will never let him go. If we fall apart, I'll do whatever I can to put us back together, even if it's in pieces. Instead of saying those things, however, I focus on the physical side and play the role he loves me in.

"I'm going to take a shower with our Duchess," I say. "And you're going to watch us."

He nods and we make our way into the bathroom where Nicole's already in the shower. The water's so hot, the place looks like a steamy sauna.

The glass shower door gives us a spectacular show of her arcing back to rinse her hair.

"Want company?"

She doesn't hesitate to respond with, "Yes."

I strip out of my clothes and step into the shower with her.

She looks up at me with big doe eyes. "Is Landon joining us too?"

"No." I flash Nicole a killer smile. "Payback's a bitch." Kissing her gently, working my way into a more dominating one, I love how she submits so easily. I spin Nicole around, smashing her tits against the glass door to give Landon a phenomenal view. "Spread your legs for me, Duchess."

There's no need to make sure Landon's watching. He wouldn't miss a show like this for anything.

I work her over, touching, kissing, and devouring every inch of her sweet skin. I hate that she's lost so much weight, but that doesn't make her any less attractive. I don't think this woman knows how to be anything other than stunning.

Instead of giving her an orgasm, I edge her until she's whimpering.

Then I shut the water off.

"You want to come so badly, don't you?"

"Yes," she whispers. Her eyes are closed, face pressed against the glass wall like it's holding her up. "I don't want to be me anymore."

My breath catches. "What's wrong with being you?"

Nicole slowly opens her eyes, and I watch her mask slide into place. "I'm cold."

"Here." Landon rips the shower door open and wraps her in a towel. "I've got you."

As he drapes her in fluffy terrycloth, I hold her gaze. I don't like the look in her eyes. It's not sultry, it's sad.

Silence blankets us while Landon dries her off. "I can do this myself," she snaps at him.

He hesitates and almost backs off, but shakes his head instead. "You aren't doing anything unless we tell you to, Duchess."

Atta boy.

I read her facial expression, calculating my next move.

When she's Nicole, she's short tempered and frustrated. When she's our Duchess, she's… something else.

"I don't want to be me anymore," she'd said in the shower.

Nicole is a loud, bold, snarky, fearless woman who has carried the weight of everyone's expectations on her shoulders. Her job is demanding and exhausting. Her family holds her to near-impossible expectations. Her circle of friends is miniscule and two-faced.

Duchess is quiet and does what she's told. Her submission isn't just a gift, it's an entirely unique existence. Her smile in that sex shop was too genuine to be an act. And the way her demeanor shifts just hearing us call her that honorific is interesting. We barely scratched the surface of this dynamic last time, and I'm suddenly determined to see how deep we can go with it.

"Get on your knees, Duchess."

Even with Landon still towel drying her hair, she obeys me.

It's fucking scary.

We loom over her like two wolves playing with a trapped bunny.

"What should we have her do now, Trick?"

"Crawl." His voice is deep and gravelly. Thick. He only ever sounds like that when he's extremely aroused.

"Good idea," I say with a smile. "Crawl, Duchess. Out of this bathroom, and into the living room. When you get to the pile of toys we bought you, stop and kneel with your hands in your lap."

She looks like a cat prowling towards dinner. So much of her body is exposed for our enjoyment that my dick is painfully hard. Landon follows her out first, and I come up behind him.

"Strip and sit across from me, Trick," I growl against his ear.

Landon does as I command, and I ease onto of one the sofas with my dick standing upright and throbbing.

Landon stalks over and sits down across from me, confusion and intrigue dancing on his face.

"Duchess, crawl over to him and lay across his lap with your ass up."

Time to get some answers.

Chapter 12

Nicole

I have no clue what they're up to, and I don't even care. Once I stretch across Landon's lap, I'm already too far gone mentally to give a shit about anything other than feeling these men touch my body.

I'm not sure what that says about me.

How do I go from a lioness in the boardroom to a kitten in the bedroom?

On our way home from the sex shop, we discussed safety precautions and a few expectations, along with the standard stuff like "teapot" being my safe word, that all three of us are still clean, and I still have my IUD. Oh, and I reiterated that I just want to get fucked into oblivion for a week.

What I didn't say was that once this week is over, I will have to kiss these two heartthrobs goodbye for good. Being with them now is dangerous enough as it is. I'm never going to recover. I just hope the damage they do, and memories we make, will be enough for me to survive on for the rest of my miserable life.

Landon runs his hand along my bare ass, making me relax.

"Why did you ghost us?" Kerrington asks from across the living room.

"That's none of your business," I snap, suddenly angry.

Smack! My ass immediately stings from the spanking Landon gives me.

"Let's try again." Kerrington leans forward. "Why did you ghost us?"

I bite my lip, unwilling to answer.

Smack! Smack!

"They will double every time you don't give us what we want," Landon warns. "Think this sweet ass can handle four more?"

Probably, but I'm not ready to find out.

"Why does it matter?" I ask.

Smack! Smack! Smack! Smack!

My head spins from the painful pleasure those spanks bring me, and I grind against his lap when he soothes the burn with his palm.

Fine. I'll confess. "I was embarrassed."

"Good girl," Landon coos.

"Why?"

I swallow the saliva building in my mouth before answering Kerrington's question. "Because I… let myself go that night."

Landon's hand slides between my thighs, probing my pussy, teasing it. "And that's a problem, how?"

I can't think straight with his fingers inside

me like this. Especially paired with the burning of ass cheeks still going strong.

"I…" Fucking hell, this feels so good. "I don't know."

"Do you like being our Duchess?" Kerrington asks while Landon fingers me slowly.

I groan with need and close my eyes to relish it.

Smack!

Eyes flying open, I yelp and try to get off of his lap. Landon's arms bracket me in place, holding me down. "Be a good girl and you won't get spanked." He shoves his finger back into me.

I could use my safe word. End this right now. But I won't.

What does that say about me?

"Every answer you give us earns you a reward, Duchess." Kerrington strokes his fat cock in front of me. He's not jerking off. He's caressing it, calmly.

My mind drifts to how I sucked on the head of Landon's soft dick earlier. I used it like a pacifier, which calmed me and that makes shame heat my face.

I don't like myself.

But I do like rewards.

I relax a little on Landon's lap. "I love being your Duchess."

"Why?" Landon asks.

"Because I feel better that way. I don't have to think. I just do what I'm told."

"You like being our good girl." Landon pushes another finger inside me. He twists them around, hitting pleasure points I can't for myself. "There we go," he coos. "Goddamn she's so wet, Kerr."

My gaze floats over to Kerrington again, and I hold his stare.

He stands slowly and walks over to our pile of toys, plucking a package off the floor. It's a remote-controlled butt plug.

"That's for Trick," I say quickly.

"I bought multiple." Kerrington unwraps the damn thing and I see it's pink. Next, he grabs a bottle of lube.

"If you don't like it, we'll stop immediately." Landon says. "What's your safe word, Duchess?"

I sigh in relief at the mere mention of my honorific. "Teapot."

"Good girl." Landon fingers me deeper, making my body turn to putty in his lap.

I watch the reflection in the window as Kerrington hands the butt plug over to Landon. Then Kerrington spreads my ass cheeks and Landon probes my tight ring of muscle while he continues to finger me with his other hand.

"Relax, baby," Kerrington's tone is so soft. "Just like last time."

Last time was Kerrington's dick in my ass. I still get off remembering how good it felt. I'd never done anal before and they worked me open so well, I could take everything they gave me. Even if it hurt to walk the next day.

I'd love to take more of them this time.

Landon eases the plug inside me, twisting and plunging it in and out a little more each time. "That's it, you're doing so good, Duchess."

His praise makes me melt, and it doesn't take long for him to work the small object inside me. Once it's seated, I remain draped across his lap, and wiggle my butt, getting used to it.

"How does it feel, baby?"

I look up at Kerrington and smile. "Nice."

He clicks a button on the remote and the plug buzzes inside me.

My fucking eyes cross.

"Oh my god," I whimper, burying my face in the couch cushion.

Landon fingers me a little faster. "Feels even better now, huh?"

"Yes." My body heats. "Fuck yes."

"Good." He works me over, making my body tense and relax, tense and relax.

"Why haven't you been eating?"

Kerrington's question throws me off track. "What?"

Smack!

Saliva floods my mouth, and I can't tell if it's from pain or pleasure, but my lower half coils with an impending vicious orgasm.

Fuck, what did he ask me? Oh yeah. "I've been too busy."

Smack! Smack!

"Oh my god! I answered your question!"

"I know," Landon says. "That's for not taking care of yourself and making sure your needs are met."

I want to cry. And there's no way I'll tell them the real reason I've deteriorated. I'm embarrassed that I look so unhealthy lately and don't have the strength to care about it anymore. My fucking *roots* are showing, for fuck's sake!

The buzzing in my ass increases.

All my brain cells vacate and the only thing I can do is grind like a mindless animal in heat against Landon's lap. Sweat blooms down my body. I feel lightheaded.

"Eyes on me, Duchess."

It takes a lot to lock gazes with Kerrington. When I do, I swear he sees through me, and I don't know what to do about it. But I don't want this pleasure to end, so I'll take the questions and answer them.

Anything for this release.

"Why aren't you taking care of yourself, Duchess?"

My orgasm is so close. Sooo. Fucking. Close. I focus on the pleasure, chasing my release, desperate for it.

And everything stops.

No buzzing. No fingering. No spanking or caressing.

Gone. It's all gone.

My heart stumbles and I gasp for air. Too many mixed emotions fly out of me at once and I scream. *"Make me come!"*

Kerrington shakes his head. "Not yet. Earn it, Nicole."

Hearing my real name is like being doused with ice water. I climb out of Landon's lap, ready to commit murder.

The buzzing in my ass starts up again, and my legs give out. Slamming to the floor, I groan and try to collect my scattered thoughts. I just want to be blown apart. I need to be messy and numb. Gone. Desperate, I crawl over to the boxes of toys and rip open the one with the rabbit. I'm so wet, it's easy to push it inside me. The batteries aren't in it, so the vibration doesn't work.

I don't care. Fucking myself harder with it, I clench my teeth and squeeze my eyes shut.

Landon leans forward, his elbows on his knees, and he arches his brow at me. "Don't you dare come yet, Duchess."

His tone makes me freeze and an awful animalistic sound rips from my throat.

I can't imagine what I must look like right now. On the floor. Naked. Sweaty. Bright red handprints all over my plugged-up ass. Arousal slick on my thighs. My cunt stuffed with a purple rabbit fresh out of a box.

I need…

"Help," I squeak as the tears finally flow. My head drops and I cry so hard, I don't even hear them approach me.

"Shh," Landon lifts me up, and the rabbit falls to the floor. The buzzing stops in my ass next. "We've got you, Nicole."

"Don't say my name," I sob.

My real name means the scene is over and I can't let this be over.

"Trick, please," I cling to him, my grip stretching out his shirt.

"Jesus Christ," he whispers. Then he looks over at Kerrington, and that makes me feel worse.

"I ran that morning because I can't have you both. And I've lost weight because I can't eat. I've worked myself into the ground, and all I do is… all I can think about is…" My heart's hammering so hard it hurts to breathe. "I just want this for a little longer. *Please.* I know I have no right to ask, and I'm sorry, but I need this."

Landon's blue eyes turn glassy and his brow furrows. "You need what exactly?"

"You," I confess. "I need *you*."

Chapter 13

Landon

Have you ever had everything you've ever wanted in your hands and then suddenly it's ripped away from you? That's what happens when Nicole says she needs me.

My heart leaps for joy a second before it shatters when I see the devastation on Kerrington's face.

I'm going to lose them both because I refuse to choose one over the other and I'm praying I will never have to. But for that dream to come true, I need to make things clear.

"Nicole," I cradle her against my chest.

"I'm sorry, and I know it's selfish, but I do. I need you." She sobs into my shirt. "I need *both* of you."

Kerrington stumbles back and the relief on his face makes me suspect that he... *holy shit...* He's in love with her, too.

He's not afraid of losing me like I am him. He was bracing to lose *her*.

How long has he been in love with her?

I wait for jealousy to rise, but it doesn't.

Kerrington told me earlier he loved me. He can love us both, right? He must.

I know I do.

Carrying Nicole into the bedroom, I lay her down on the mattress and quietly ask her to, "Relax for me so I can take this toy out."

She covers her face with her hands like she's ashamed, and that's the last thing I want her to feel.

"It's okay," I say, carefully pulling the plug out and handing it over to Kerrington for him to take care of. "Hey, come here." I wrap her in a warm embrace and stroke her hair. "We're here and we're not going anywhere. Shh."

Kerrington quietly returns and sits on the edge of the bed. He looks at both of us and his face goes a little blank. I don't like it.

"If you need us both…" I say to Nicole, even though I'm staring at Kerrington, "You can have us both."

I dare him to challenge me on this.

His throat bobs as he swallows, and we exchange a million silent words while I hold Nicole in my arms.

"I just want that night back," she cries into my chest. "I need it back."

I'm no time traveler, but I can certainly get us back to the way we were that night. "Okay, Duchess." My body locks in on one mission. "Lay back for us."

Still covered in tears, she does what I say.

I'm not a fool. This is probably a bad time to get into a sex scene, but I'm not going to pump the brakes just yet. I strip out of my clothes, then position myself between her legs. "You still want to be our fucktoy, Duchess?"

"Yes, please."

"Such good manners," Kerrington chimes in. He crawls up to the headboard and teases her mouth with the tip of his dick. It's not hard anymore, but that'll change fast. "Suck," he orders.

She takes him into her mouth and sucks. Her body becomes more pliable. Her breaths mellow out.

"That's it, Duchess." Hovering over her, he lets her suck his cock like it's a soothing mechanism. She did that to me earlier, and I gotta say it was fucking nice.

"I think our pretty girl has earned an orgasm, don't you, Trick?"

"Fuck yeah, she has." I lick her pussy. Arousal coats my tongue with the first drag across her cunt, and I'm addicted immediately.

Duchess reaches up and strokes Kerrington's dick while she spreads her legs wider for me and runs her other hand through my hair. She enjoys us both simultaneously.

It's that easy.

"Careful, baby," Kerrington warns. "I'm not going to stay soft much longer and you might not like how I fuck your throat."

We all know she'll love it.

"Give me," she begs, pumping his length.

"Fuuuuck." Kerrington repositions on top of her and feeds her his hardening cock. We face each other while I lick her cunt and he fucks her face, both of us taking our time to enjoy every sensation that runs through us.

"You're next," Kerrington tells me.

Nicole groans, hearing him say that, and her hips lift so she can grind against my face harder.

I don't want this to be about me tonight. I want Nicole drained and passed the fuck out. Sucking her clit in fast bursts, I wring the first orgasm out of her in no time. She bucks against my face and Kerrington's dick blocks her screams when she orgasms. I love how her thighs shake when she clamps them around my head.

"Give her another, Trick. That one came too fucking easy."

My pleasure. But it won't be like this. "Pull out."

Kerrington pops out of her mouth and jacks himself off. I immediately drag Nicole off the bed by her ankles. "Squat and spread your legs as far as you can stand it."

Her cheeks are flushed. When she does what I say, I shove two fingers in her cunt and am absolutely ruthless with how I make her orgasm again. "Next time we do this, Kerrington's fucking your ass."

"O...k-k-kay." She can barely hold her

balance as she tips onto the balls of her feet and keeps her thighs spread wide open. She whines and whimpers while she takes what I give her. The squelching noises start up and in less than a minute, I have her squirting. She screams something incoherent, and I tap her bare pussy hard and fast, spanking it just to play with her a little more. "Such a pretty fucktoy you are."

Sweat makes her hair stick to her face. She's still gasping for air when Kerrington loops his arms under hers and drags her back onto the bed with him again.

I crawl after them both like a dog. "You taste so fucking good, Duchess." I lick the mess from between her thighs.

God*damn* that's delicious.

"Trick," she whines. "Holy shit, I can't feel my face."

Kerrington holds her against his chest, his legs spread to make room for her body, and he collars her throat with one hand, while he rubs her clit with the other. "Come on baby, give us another."

His fingers make fast work of bringing her to a third climax. She's wheezing, screaming, and clawing at the sheets now. "Oh *God!*"

I hold her legs open while he makes her have another release. Nicole's head tips back on his shoulder and she cries out. Tears spill down her face as she rides her climax, and all I can do is watch in awe.

"Such a good girl," Kerrington growls against her ear. "Look at the pretty mess you are."

She's so exhausted, her eyes are barely open.

I swipe the hair from her face and kiss her while Kerrington keeps her flush against his body. "Feel better now, Duchess?"

Nicole nods.

"Words, baby." Kerrington kisses her shoulder. "We need your voice."

"Yes," she croaks out, then clears her throat. "Thank you."

We're the ones who should thank her. This is a fucking treat.

"Now you," she slurs. "It's your turn."

I'm not sure she can handle much more of us tonight. It's clear she's been through something that's taken a huge toll on her and the stamina she had last time might not be here anymore. But…

"Kiss," she says in this little voice that makes my heart pound.

"Well, you were a very good girl, giving us what we wanted and coming so beautifully." I lift her off Kerrington and he helps me tuck her into the bed. "I think we can give you a reward."

"Use your manners first," Kerrington chides.

"Please kiss Trick for me, Daddy."

Ffffuuuuuuck. That wasn't manners. That was voodoo.

My body immediately reacts viscerally to it, and I can't seem to make my brain and mouth connect.

"You get to see us kiss once and then you're going to bed. Do you understand?"

"Yes, Daddy."

My cock is so hard right now I think I could blow my load from a slight breeze hitting it.

Kerrington crooks his finger at me and I lean forward so he can wrap his hand around my throat. I love when he's aggressive. And I love hearing Nicole call him Daddy.

I think a new kink just unlocked for me.

Kerr closes in on me slowly and when our mouths meet, I'm pulled into his gravity, like always. This man owns me. And I wouldn't have it any other way. Our tongues dance together as we give and take. When I pull back first, he sucks on my bottom lip and a groan escapes me.

I want to fuck.

"Was that what you wanted, baby?" Kerrington's question is, I think, for Nicole, but he's staring at me.

"Yes," she says in a lazy tone. "Thank you."

"You're welcome. Now close your eyes and sleep."

We leave her to drift off alone in the bedroom. Once the door shuts, Kerrington lets out a long sigh. "I don't think I can do this."

"What?"

"I can't do this, Landon."

He runs his hands angrily through his hair and my stomach drops.

"What do you mean? You said we could give her the week."

"I don't want a week!" he screams at me. Then he squeezes his eyes shut and tries to calm the fuck down. "I don't… want… a week."

"Then what do you want?"

Instead of answering me, he storms out of the room and heads to our private balcony. "I need air."

Chapter 14

Kerrington

I stayed out on the balcony long enough for my balls to freeze last night. Landon never came out with me, which is unusual, but not completely surprising. I don't know how to tell him what I feel, and I'm scared to death I'm fucking all of this up because I can't communicate properly.

But how do I explain to the man I love that I'm also in love with a woman? How do I tell him I've felt inferior my whole life and that he's the only person who makes me feel worthy of love and that I want to share that love with another person who isn't him? How do I admit that I need them both when I don't deserve either?

It's obvious he cares for her too, but it's foolish to believe we can have a life together, all three of us, because Nicole would never go for it. She said it herself; she was embarrassed. She'd let herself go that night. As if being her authentic self is some kind of crime?

It hurt like hell to hear her say that, but I get it. She's from a different life, and her family is always in some kind of spotlight. The press would likely eat her alive for having two men at her beck and call. Society is unkind about anything outside of what they deem "the norm."

Besides, Nicole's not in this for the long ride. She's giving us one week.

One. Motherfucking. Week.

I want forever.

Lying next to her in bed, with Landon on her other side, I watch the two of them sleep. The sunrise filters pale-yellow light into our room, making Landon's sun kissed skin even more golden. I memorize every slope and crest of their two bodies entwined. When I reach their faces, I see Landon staring at me.

"I love you too," he says in a soft, sleepy voice.

My heart stops beating.

"Always have, Kerr. Always will." He wraps his arm around Nicole's middle and kisses her shoulder. "She changes nothing."

She changes *everything*. Why can't he see that?

"I can't let her go," I say against my better judgment. Having this discussion at the ass crack of dawn is not the way it should be done. But I've wasted too much time stewing in my madness to let it continue for another minute.

"I can't either," he says, shocking me.

My hand trembles when I place it over his. I don't know why I feel this fucking weak and scared. But the two people who own my heart and soul are in this bed with me and I cannot stand the idea of us not being together for the rest of our lives. "These past six months have been…"

"Hard without her."

I nod. "But she doesn't take your place, Lan. She never could."

"I know that." He flashes me a tired smile. It's cautious and guarded. I hate it.

"I mean it." Crawling carefully around Nicole, I straddle Landon and pin his hands above his head. "I cannot lose you and she is not a replacement."

He swallows hard and stares at me. "Is she the reason you've been so distant with me lately?"

"Maybe." I'm not even sure. I just know that the minute I saw her again, I felt connected to this other part of me I've missed. "Is she the reason you've been so difficult lately?"

"Maybe."

"Are you in love with her?"

He stills under me. I glance over to see Nicole's still knocked out. Her mouth is parted slightly, and her breaths are deep and even. Good. I'm glad she's found peace and safety between us and can catch up on her rest. That's how it should always be.

I bring my attention back to Landon and cock my brow, waiting for his admission.

He nods, the vein in his throat pulsing

rapidly.

"I'm in love with her too," I finally admit out loud. Guilt assaults me and I pull away, needing fresh air again. Leaving them in bed, I yank the balcony door open and am smacked with freezing cold temperatures and the whirr of traffic below.

At least I'm not naked anymore.

Landon's warm hand runs along my spine, and I close my eyes, inwardly cringing. "You don't have to pick, Kerr."

"Why does it feel like I do?"

"Because you're an idiot."

That makes me laugh a little. "Landon, I don't know why this is so hard. All my feelings… all my thoughts…" I grab the back of his neck and press our foreheads together. "You consume me."

"And so does she."

My stomach twists because he's right.

"It's okay to want more than me, Kerr."

I don't want it. I *need* it. And that's not something I'll ever say out loud. It'll hurt him. "I don't deserve you."

"Why would you say some shit like that?"

"Because you should have someone who matches your energy. Gives you everything you've ever wanted. Shows you every day that you mean the world to them."

"And that's not you?" He steps away from me as if I've hit him.

"I'm not good at this stuff. I should show

you how I feel all the time."

"You groped my dick at the sex shop. I mean, honestly, if we're going for gold here, you win."

"That's not the same and you know it." He's making light of this because he's scared. I am too. "How long?"

"How long what?"

"Have you been in love with Nicole?" I turn to look at him again, holding my breath.

He shrugs with his hands out. "Since college graduation."

My god, we're both fucking idiots. "I think I fell in love with her that night we played poker and she had you stripped naked and handing over your Rolex."

"Ahh, junior year then. Wow." Landon drops into a chair and scrubs his face. "So, we've been pining over the same fucking woman for a long goddamn time."

"Guess so."

"I always kind of knew, you know." He blows out a long sigh. "That you had feelings for her."

My heart does this horrible blur-blub thing that makes me queasy. "How so?"

"The way you always look at her." Landon's gaze lifts to mine, arresting me. "It's the same way you look at me."

Fuuuuck.

Silence falls like snow around us. The sun

rises higher, bouncing light everywhere.

"We're not going to let her go this time," he announces. "We're keeping her."

"She's not a rescue animal, Lan."

"No. She's our Duchess."

"She has a life to get back to. One that she's cut us out of, I might add."

"Then we build her a new one with us. Show her how amazing it is to be loved by two men at the same time."

"She doesn't want love. She wants to be fucked into another timeline."

"Well, we can do that too." Landon stands up like it's a done deal. "She's not leaving us again, Kerrington."

"We don't have a say in it."

"She loves us too."

Now he's certifiable. "Landon. You're reaching." And I hate the way my heart swells, hoping he's possibly right.

"She came here for us."

"She went to Mason."

"Because she knew we were going there to see him."

"If she wanted us, she'd have called or showed up at our doorstep, not his."

"He's her safe space," Landon reminds me. "Even when they want to kill one another, they've always been there for each other. That gala showed how deep their love is."

And how fucked up their families are.

Mason and Nicole's prearranged marriage was a huge reason I never touched Nicole until that night. I don't know what I would have done if they'd gone through with the nuptials. I'd have a miserable best friend married to the woman I don't think I can live without.

And Landon would suffer in silence the whole time, too, putting on a brave face and keeping his true feelings about her hidden from me for the rest of our lives.

Is that the same as living a lie, or is it living half a life?

I squeeze my eyes shut and let that sink in. "What do we have to do to keep her?"

"Well, we can either make her fall madly in love with both of us, or, hear me out, we can chain her up in the basement. I'm cool with either."

"We don't have a basement." A laugh bubbles out of me because, oh my god, this motherfucker is deranged in the best of ways. "How about we start with that collar and short leash?"

"Give her what she wants, so she sees what she'll be missing if she walks away again."

"Precisely."

"And if that doesn't work?"

"I'll buy duct tape, two masks, some rope…. and a house with a goddamn basement."

"Atta boy." Landon pats me on the back and swings the door open, ushering me inside. "Hey."

"Hmmm?" I turn to him again with this

stabbing pain in my chest.

"You deserve me," he says, kissing my forehead. "And you deserve her, too."

With that, Landon walks away and leaves me with my heart splattered on the floor.

Chapter 15

Warm and cozy.
Full and good.
So good.
So full…
Wait.

My brain slips as it tries to connect with what's happening to my body.

Reaching between my legs, I feel a head of thick hair moving, soft lips kissing my inner thighs and a tongue licking me.

"Kerrington."

His hair is shorter than Landon's, which is the only way I can tell it's him. He's buried beneath the sheets, waking me up in the best of ways.

I swallow, suddenly noticing a slight pressure around my neck. It takes a second to realize I'm in my pretty pink collar. Damn, how hard did I sleep last night?

Kerrington pulls the bedsheets off of us and has the end of my leash wound around his hand. He sits up and pulls the chain, making me rise to meet him.

"Good afternoon, Duchess."

Words cannot describe how hot this man is. I think I could get used to waking up like this every day. "Hi."

He jerks my leash, pitching me forward until my mouth collides with his. I push back instinctively because I haven't brushed my teeth yet. "Wait. Eww. Let me freshen up first."

"The only thing I'm going to *let* you do… is come." He rolls me over so that I'm straddling him. "Climb up here, Duchess."

Is he serious? "Umm."

"Sit on my face."

"Wait. I really need to wash up. I'm still a mess from last night."

He jerks my chain as if silently scolding me. Correcting me.

My pussy clenches in approval. Oh my god, what is wrong with me?

Kerrington cocks his brow and stares at me, waiting for me to listen. I wonder what he'd do if I disobeyed? "I don't want to come right now."

Rejection dances in his eyes, but he quickly hides it. "Duchess, if you don't do what you're told, there will be consequences."

"But I don't want to come yet. I want to make you come… *Daddy*."

Using that honorific has always been a fantasy of mine and I'm so happy Kerrington allows me to call him that. It suits him perfectly.

"Will that make you happy?"

I run my hands up and down his chest. He's fully clothed, and I'm naked, which seems to be a theme with us lately. "Yes."

"If it'll make you happy, then put your mouth on me."

The way he gives me permission to suck him off turns me on tremendously.

Fumbling with his shorts, I pull them down, loving how his hard dick springs free. Wrapping my hand around it, I pull his skin taut and run my nails up and down his shaft.

His head tips back on my pillow and he sucks in a harsh breath. "That feels amazing."

Pride swells in my chest because I love pleasing him. I want him to feel good.

With a smirk, he pulls my leash, leading me down to his groin. "Can I come in your mouth?"

"Definitely." I lick his tip, teasing him. Then I suck him down as far as I can and use my hand to stroke him at the same time. He's hot on my tongue. Smooth. Fat. My jaw aches after a while, but I like it.

"You're doing so good, Duchess." Placing a hand on my head, he guides my pace, and drool drips all over his cock and my hand. "You ready for me, baby?"

"Mm hmm."

"Don't stop." His breaths turn harsher. "Fuuuuck, don't stop. That's it. I'm so close, Duchess. Gonna come down that dainty little throat of yours."

My leash rattles as I suck him off. My pussy is so wet I can feel moisture between my thighs. Kerrington grabs a chunk of my hair and groans with his release. Salty sweetness floods my tastebuds, and I swallow greedily, keeping him in my mouth until he turns flaccid.

I love sucking their dicks when they're soft like this. There's no real reason why other than it feels nice and makes my frenzied brain calm down a little.

"Such a good girl," he says in a ragged tone, running his hand over my head. "Fuuuuck you're incredible, Duchess."

"Mmph."

"Do you like having my cock in your pretty little mouth?"

"Mmm hmm."

He relaxes and lets me do my thing until I'm ready to release him. Cleaning the corners of my mouth, I make sure to get every drop of his climax while he watches me with a hooded gaze.

The sound of a door closing confuses me.

Landon.

"Well, I see I've missed all the fun." He fake pouts from the doorway.

"We just got started." Kerrington pitches me forward, so I'm straddling his waist. "Our Duchess wanted to make me come."

"Very generous of you, sweetheart." Landon makes his way forward, holding a little black bag from his finger. "But before we continue with breakfast, second breakfast, elevensies, lunch, and so on, I got you something."

It feels weird accepting a gift from Landon while I can still taste Kerrington's cum in my mouth. I can't tell if I feel sexy or disgraceful.

Stop it, Nicole.

"Open it." Landon hands me the bag.

Biting my bottom lip, I pull out a small velvet box and pop the lid. A pair of stunning sapphire earrings sparkle at me. "They're gorgeous. But why on earth did you buy me these?"

"If you're going to be Free Use for us, there needs to be boundaries. We can't just assume you're game to be our fucktoy for the entire week." Landon sits on the edge of the bed and tucks my hair behind my ear. "Wear these when you want to be a toy. Take them off when you want something else."

"What about what *you* want?"

Landon and Kerrington exchange a look I can't decipher.

"This week isn't about us. It's about you, baby." Kerrington runs his hands up and down my thighs.

I climb off him and tuck my legs under my ass at the corner of the bed opposite Landon. "Why?"

"Because it's what you want," Landon

answers like I've asked a stupid question.

"You wanted to be our Duchess for the week. You said you wanted to be…"

"I know what I said!" My heart won't stop beating in my throat. I feel sick. Clutching the earrings, the urge to chuck them at his head is strong. But I reel in my anger because he doesn't know what he doesn't know. Me getting mad that he can't read my mind is immature and ridiculous. And since I'm not willing to open up and say what's weighing on my heart, I have to accept that this is all I'm going to get out of them.

A weeklong dickdown and a pair of fucking earrings.

"Thank you," I say, schooling my tone. With shaky hands, I pull the earrings out and put them on. "How do they look?"

Neither of them answer me quick enough.

Frustrated with myself, I slip off the bed and storm into the bathroom, slamming the door shut.

What the fuck is the matter with me? I'm being a bitch. A slut. A greedy little whore. Selfish in a million ways.

Weak.

"Snap out of it, Nicole." I pat my cheeks and look at my reflection.

Oh. My. God.

My mascara's got me rocking raccoon energy. The goddamn collar around my neck is mocking me and the leash is dangling like my morals. Right between my tits. Gone are my curves and soft belly. I've got more ribs poking out than a motherfucking BBQ contest, and my skin is pale and horrid.

How could Landon and Kerrington be attracted to me?

Easy. They're not. They're just appeasing me because I'm a hole to fuck. An easy lay.

A desperate, shameful cunt who needs a fix and they're more than happy to fill the roles.

Tears sting my eyes. I think I'm going to throw up.

I can't believe I've done this. There's no reason to be mad at anyone but myself here. They're giving me exactly what I asked for. A week in their beds, as their Duchess.

I bet they felt this same pity for me the night of the gala.

They never showed interest in me before then. *Never.* Sometimes I'd think I'd catch Kerrington staring at me, but it was easy to dismiss as a delusion. All because I was crazy for him didn't mean he's felt the same in return. And Landon? That man would flirt with roadkill. It's just who he is. Fun, filthy, and carefree to a fault.

Neither of them thinks I'm special. And I'm not some pick-me girl who would try to get them to fall for me.

No matter how many times I've fantasized about it.

The morning after the gala, I ran out of their lives and as far as I could get from the fantasy we conjured and didn't give myself a chance to be weak again. I deleted all the social media apps off my phone and hired someone to post for me instead. Next, I went into damage control at work and home.

My parents have too much control over me and my money. I work my ass off for our family's corporation and it's taken a toll on me. Hence the ribcage and bags under my eyes.

And the nervous breakdown I had the night before I packed my bags and headed to Mason and Leah's.

This is my rock bottom.

Who would have thought it came with a collar and short leash?

And two men who have big dicks and even bigger hearts?

It's unfair to put them in this position. I should have stayed away. And yet... I've gaslighted myself into believing that they want me too. Even if it's just for the week. I've managed to fully convince myself that they're happy to have me in their bed and at their pleasure mercy.

Fucking Hell. What am I doing?

"Nicole?" Kerrington raps softly on the door. "Can I come in?"

"Just a minute!" Shit. I need to clean myself up. "Give me five more minutes."

"Take all the time you need, baby."

Baby. Why does it feel so nice when he calls me *baby*?

Goddamnit, this is horrible. I tried to escape Hell and ended up in the seventh circle of it with not one, but two handsome devils.

What would Mason do?

That's been my motto for years. What would Mason do? He's got life all figured out and has since college. While I was up there visiting him so I could see his best friends again—because it sure as shit wasn't to see him, ew—I grew more and more envious of his bold outlook and give-no-fucks lifestyle.

Shit, the man's got a billion dollars, is marrying the love of his life—who is an extremely successful camgirl, by the way—and has carved a perfect, new path for himself.

I want that too.

He didn't care about what people thought. Not even after the press had a field day over our prearranged marriage getting called off or that he was dating a camgirl who doubled as his house cleaner. Now he's helping her solidify a brand-new business that's sure to take the sex industry by storm. The Brazen Bunny will make them a gazillion dollars because sex sells, and Mason nor Leah have any shame about their lifestyle.

Must be nice.

God, Leah has no clue how lucky she is to have Mason by her side.

What I wouldn't give for a piece of that kind of devotion and support.

In my world, men rule, and women need to

stay quiet unless they're told otherwise. The fact that my father put me in a power role at his company didn't help. I have to be double vicious or else. And the night I had with Kerrington and Landon got out and was posted on social media platforms everywhere.

It must have cost my parents a fortune to have it erased.

My relationship with my mother and father was barely functional before, and now it's beyond resentful. They're stuck with a daughter who is a disgrace. I'm stuck with a family who I can never live up to. They don't care that this life is killing me. They don't care that I'm miserable.

In fact, I heard my mother and her friends talking about how I did something wrong if Mason would rather marry a camgirl instead of me.

It didn't matter that he and I never wanted it or that we practically hated each other all our lives because we knew we'd be stuck together. It didn't matter that he was in love with Leah. It didn't matter that I have feelings. It didn't matter that my one night with two men was better than a lifetime with anyone else.

My parents just put me to task, sending me all over the globe for their corporation's benefit.

They let people call me names under their breath.

They're ashamed of me. All because I wanted to be happy for one motherfucking night.

With trembling hands, I take out the earrings and pause.

Why… *fuck*…. Why can't I just be happy for a little longer? Being their toy means giving them both a gift. *I'm* a gift. And the exchange between us is even and valid. We're all getting something great out of this dynamic. Temporarily, yes, but it's still real.

And it'll have to be enough to last me forever.

So, I keep the earrings in. I brush my goddamn teeth. I shower and pull on a robe. Then I open the door to face my demons head on.

Chapter 16

Landon

"I've fucked up."

"No, you haven't." Kerrington sits on the edge of the bed. "She's just going through something we don't understand."

"Did you see her face? She's ashamed."

"We'll help her work through it."

"Some things can't be solved in a week. This is one of them, Kerr." But what other choice do we have? She's put a time limit on us, for fuck's sake. "I thought the earrings were a perfect compromise. Instead, I've made her feel cheap."

"You did no such thing." Kerrington climbs out of the bed and pulls his pants up. "If anything, I did. She sucked my dick and then…" His words fade into silence. "The earrings were perfect. You're right. She needs a way to signal us when she wants something and when she doesn't. I can't bear the thought of using her like a whore twenty-four-seven."

"Same." But then something occurs to me. *Shit.* "What if that's what *she* wants, though?" Closing the space between us, I drop my voice to a whisper. "What if that's all she wants from us? To be used up like a whore?"

My dick hardens at the thought.

Jesus fucking Christ, I need to get a grip. What's wrong with me?

Before we can discuss it further, the bathroom door swings open, and Nicole steps out in a bathrobe that's too big and her hair wet and dripping.

But her earrings are still in.

And if my dick dares to leap for joy about it, I might just cut it off.

"Sit," Kerrington says, going into Dom mode immediately.

Our Duchess saunters over to the bed and plops down. I'm momentarily shocked speechless as she stares at up at him, waiting for his next command.

Making my way over to her, I keep my tone level and stern, because she has two Doms at her beck and call. "Talk to us."

"About what?"

"You know what, Duchess." Kneeling, I gently spread her thighs with my hands. "Answer us. Good girls get rewarded, remember? Are you going to be our good girl?"

"Or our nasty little whore?" Kerrington adds.

Nicole licks her lips, likely trying to figure out the answer she thinks we want to hear.

"You can be both," I say, untying her robe.

She scoffs. "How can I be both?"

This woman has a lot to learn about love. "We'll teach you."

"You being Duchess means you're *ours*." Kerrington inches closer. "Ours to take care of. Ours to love and protect."

Her eyes widen with what looks like fear and worry. "You mean I'm yours to fuck."

"Wrong." I slap her pussy.

Nicole yelps and slams her legs shut. "Hey!"

"Open." I pry her thighs apart with little effort. "Now repeat after us."

Kerrington climbs onto the bed, positioning himself behind her, and gathers her wet hair in his hand. "I'm yours."

Nicole's mouth clamps shut. She looks like she's about to cry.

"Do I need to spank this pussy again?" My threat makes her nostrils flare.

"I…" She huffs, exasperated. "I'm yours."

Skating my fingers up and down her thighs, I bring her attention to me. "I'm yours to take care of."

Tears well in her sparkling hazel eyes. "I'm yours to take care of."

"I'm yours to protect and love."

She freezes at Kerrington's words. Her eyes are still locked onto mine, and I nod, hoping it's enough encouragement. Her chin trembles as her mouth parts open. "I'm… I'm yours to…"

Lacing my hands with hers, I give them a

squeeze and keep eye contact. "Keep going. You're doing great."

A runaway tear rolls down her cheek. "I'm yours to protect…"

"And?" Kerrington pulls the robe off her shoulders and kisses the side of her neck. "Finish that sentence, Duchess."

"And yours to love."

Her voice cracks when she says that, and my fucking heart shatters.

"That's right, baby. And we're going to take very good care of you." Kerrington tips her chin and kisses her softly.

She whimpers against his mouth.

Of all the things I've seen and heard so far that's let me know she's hurting, this is by far the worst. Our girl has been in torment, and we haven't been there to stop it or to ease her suffering. That ends today.

"We want more than a week," I confess. "We want forever."

Nicole's thighs start closing, but I block her with my body. "Don't shut us out again, Nicole."

Another tear escapes and runs down her face.

"I can't stay," she says. "I have to go back in six days."

"Back to what? Misery?" Kerrington slips her robe off. "Hell? A life that is someone else's instead of your own?"

"Stay with us," I beg on my knees. "Be with

us, Nicole."

A guttural noise rips from her throat, and she cries harder. "I can't."

"Yes, you can." I lean up and kiss her sweet mouth. "You absolutely can."

"We love you," Kerrington confesses for us both. "We have for a very, very long time."

She gasps, shaking her head as if we've said something that can't be unheard.

There's no amount of refusal that will knock it out of her memory now. I hope our revelation burns into her soul.

"We've suffered without you," I say, pressing kisses to her cheeks and the tip of her nose. "We aren't the same without you."

"It was one night," she cries. "It was only supposed to be *one night*."

"No." Kerrington runs his hands up and down her arms. "It's supposed to be every night. All the nights. And all the days."

"We've wasted precious time." My body relaxes when Kerrington puts his hand over mine and we touch our girl together. "No more games, Nicole. No more running. No more being ashamed and hiding."

"Be with us." Kerrington nuzzles her neck and kisses her jawline.

"I..." The rejection is on the tip of her tongue, so I suck on it until I'm kissing her hard enough to press her backwards into Kerrington's chest.

Pulling back for a breather, I cup her face and say, "Give us a chance to show you what life would be like with us. If you want to leave after that, we won't stop you and we'll never ask again."

She goes rigid and stops breathing. I'm not sure if I've said the wrong thing again or not. But she inevitably wraps her arms around my neck, pulling me into her orbit, and accepts our offer. "Okay."

"Yes?"

"Yes, I'll let you show me."

Victory has never tasted sweeter than our next kiss. I have one hand on Kerrington's thigh, the other cupping Nicole's face. My mind glitches. All the worries plaguing me vanish like little bubbles popping, one by one.

I think we're smothering her, but she doesn't seem to mind.

"Tell us what you want," I whisper against her lips. Even the bedroom seems to hold its breath, scared that one wrong move will shatter everything. "Say it and it's done."

"I..." Nicole's eyes roll back when Kerrington palms her tits and pinches her nipples. "I want you to fuck me. At the same time."

"How?" Kerrington growls, tugging her nipples a little harder.

She gasps with a grin, even with her eyes shut. "I want you both in my pussy."

DVP is no joke. We'll have to be careful, so she doesn't tear.

"Let's work up to that, baby." Kerrington nips her earlobe. "You'll have to be a very good girl to earn our cocks like that."

He's right, but also, we have to prep her for a while. Work our way up to it. She's ours to protect, right? That means making sure what we do with her body is always safe.

"Don't worry, we'll definitely get there," Kerrington says. "But we're going to go slow and do other things with you first. Do you understand?"

"Mmph." She grinds against Kerrington while I play with her pussy. "Yes, Daddy."

Aaaaand just like that, I almost blow in my fucking pants.

How is this so hot?

"That's our good girl." I dip down and lick her cunt. "You like getting rewards, don't you, Duchess?"

"Yes." Her hand sinks into my hair. "And I like making you happy."

Something aggressive stirs inside me. I don't want her to make me happy. I want her to make *herself* happy. "Do you know what I want?"

"What?" she asks, a little too eager to please me.

"I want you to tell me how to make you come."

Giving her all the power is easy. Effortless.

"I want you to fuck me while Kerrington watches. And when we're done... I want him to suck my cum off your dick."

Be still my horny little heart. "You good with that, Kerr?"

Fuck yeah, he is. Just look at the way his jaw clenches and eyes darken. "Yeah. Definitely."

Elated, I give him a second to climb out of the bed and have a seat over in the chair by the window. He leans back, clutching the armrests, and watches us with eager anticipation.

Smiling big, I turn my attention back to Nicole. "Did you suck him off already today, Duchess?"

"Yes." She looks proud about it. "And I swallowed all his cum."

"Good girl." I pull off my shirt. "That earns you a reward." Unbuckling my belt, I pull my jeans down and kick them off. "You pick the position."

"Doggie," she answers without hesitation.

Grabbing her ankles, I drag her to the corner of the bed and slap her ass. "Spread them."

She presents her holes to me like an offering.

Kerrington lets out a long exhale and I'm sure he's dying for a taste. Too bad. She's all mine right now. "Do you hear how turned on Kerrington is, Duchess?"

She nods.

"Use your words." I spread her ass cheeks even more.

"Yes."

"Do you like making him desperate for you?"

"Yes."

"Good girl." I push a finger inside her pussy. "Goddamn you're so slick right now."

Kerrington lets out the tiniest of moans.

"He wants to taste this pussy so fucking bad." I slap her ass. "But it belongs to me." I spank her again, giving her matching handprints on both cheeks. "So. Fucking. Gorgeous."

Fisting my dick, I press the head of it against her cunt and tease her. "Beg, whore."

"Please fuck me."

That was way too easy. Running my fingers through her pussy, I coat them in her arousal, then play with her asshole, rimming it, probing it. "Beg harder."

"Mmph. Please, fuck me, Trick. I need your cock inside me."

"Where do you want me come?"

"Inside me." She tries to push back against my groin, and I spank her again.

"Be more specific, Duchess." I run my finger along her tight ring of muscle. "In your ass?" I rub my dick along her pussy. "In this swollen cunt?" Then I grab her throat from behind, forcing her to tip backwards until she's flush against me. "Or in this perfectly fuckable mouth?"

Nicole's panting now and we haven't even started.

"My body. Paint my body with it."

It's okay to have changed her mind about wanting it inside her. I'll unload anywhere she desires. "Whatever you want, Duchess."

Letting her throat go, I let her fall forward and then I mount up. It makes me feel like a rutting beast in this position, and I love it. "You're going to take it all, aren't you?"

"Yes."

"That's our good little whore."

She groans as I push my way inside her pussy, an inch at a time. When I bottom out, she gasps and claws the bedding.

"Too much?"

"N-no." She breathes faster. "Just let me adjust."

I'm a lot to take, so I get it. The best way to adjust is to keep moving or it'll hurt. Running my hands over her cherry red ass, I pull out a little and thrust back inside her with some force. "You're taking me so well, Duchess."

Within no time, she's molded to me, taking everything I have to give. My thrusts quicken. The sounds of our bodies slapping together are loud in my ears. Kerrington watches us like a hawk, and I know he's loving the show.

Who wouldn't?

"Get our girl a toy," I command.

Kerr unfolds from the chair and disappears behind us, coming back a moment later with a wand.

I turn it on the lowest setting and reach around to press it against her clit. Her back is already clammy with sweat, and she won't stop meeting each of my thrusts with her own. "Fuck, Trick!"

"You're going to keep it on there until I tell you otherwise." Pressing her down on the mattress, I sandwich her between me and the vibrator. She can't move with me on top like this. She just has to take it. "That's a good girl." I deepen my thrusts. My cock is coated in her cream. Her body goes rigid. "That's it. Fucking come all over me, slut. I want to feel you squeeze around my dick."

Nicole buries her face in the bedding and screams. She barely has room to wiggle beneath me, and I keep her pinned while I fuck her senseless. She orgasms three times before she starts crying happy tears.

"Give me one more. I know you can." I'm so close to my own orgasm, but I'm not giving in until I can wring one more from her sweet body.

"Trick!" She tries to lift off, and I grip her hips, holding her in place.

"Give it to me."

Her body shakes hard under me. A glorious sound rips from her throat, and I pull out, jacking off until I unload all over her ass cheeks and lower back. Meanwhile, she grinds against the wand, pressing into the mattress, riding a final wave of glory with zero qualms about how filthy she looks doing it.

"You did so good for us," I say, pulling the vibrator out from between her thighs. She makes this little mewling sound that has me ready for another round, but first… "Stay just like this."

I don't think she can hear me. Nicole's still grinding her lower half into the mattress. She must still be riding the aftershocks of that last one. Good.

Crooking my finger at Kerr, I signal him to join us. "Clean her off."

He arches his brow at me. "Together."

Fine by me.

We both lower down and lick my cum off Nicole's backside. She squeals and groans while we clean her off. Kerrington runs his hands all over her first, then me. I grab his neck and kiss him with my taste on us both.

"She wants you to taste her," I remind him.

Kerrington lowers down to me while I rise on my knees, holding my dick out for him. Nicole rolls over so she can watch. I'm torn between who I should look at, so I close my eyes because I can't choose.

Kerr's mouth is hot. But the hands cupping my balls are chilled.

I look down to see them working together to worship me. "She tastes divine, doesn't she?"

"Ambrosia for the gods," Kerr answers. Then he kisses Nicole deeply and when they pull away, they've got these lazy big smiles on their faces.

A thousand emotions swirl inside my chest, making my heart stop.

I will *never* give this up again.

No matter what it costs me.

Chapter 17

Nicole

I must be out of my goddamn mind. It's Landon's fault. He can't just dick me down so good that all my worries and shame evaporate.

It's a cock. Not a cure.

What is wrong with me?

Still, I can't seem to care about anything other than the way they work together to make me feel like I'm the purest form of pleasure on earth.

Kerrington kisses me like I'm better than the air he breathes.

Landon touches me like I'm a drug he'll never get out of his system.

If I leave…. Will one suffocate and the other collapse?

My heart sinks because I don't want them to suffer. Ever. The things they confessed earlier roll through me, making me cautious about my next move.

They said they love me.

"Is that really true?" I'm too stupid to stop the words from leaving my dumb mouth.

"Is what true, baby?" Kerrington's got me tucked into his chest while Landon's lying on my other side, running idle circles along my thigh. The post orgasmic bliss has all of us rocking lazy house cat energy.

"That you love me."

Oh my god, why am I being so pathetic? I shouldn't ask. I should have just stayed quiet and let them touch me.

Kerrington lifts his head, scowling. "Do you think we'd lie about something like that, Nicole?"

And now, of course, my mouth decides not to work.

"We don't play with feelings," Landon pipes up. "And we'd never say something that wasn't true."

"You don't even know me," I finally get out.

"How can you say that?" Kerrington grabs my hand and kisses my knuckles. "You're strong and smart and sassy as fuck."

Landon swipes the hair from my face and kisses my forehead. "You've been in the spotlight your whole life."

"You love spicy food." Kerrington brings my attention back to him. "And you have a terrible habit of acting like you hate people because it's your coping mechanism."

Guilty.

Inwardly, I cringe. "You've forgotten the most crucial thing."

"What's that?" Landon hooks his arm

around my middle and nuzzles against me.

"That I'm a callous bitch with no soul."

Kerrington pinches my chin, a look of disdain clear on his handsome face. "Don't ever let me catch you calling yourself that again, Nicole. Understand me?"

I swallow around the tightness in my throat. "It's hard to see myself any other way when that's all I'm used for."

Landon lifts onto his elbow and props his head. "You're a shark in bloody waters. That's the nature of your business."

The way he says it almost makes my actions excusable. "I tear apart companies, paying them pennies on the dollar for their life's work. I basically rip apart their hopes and dreams."

"You bail them out of bankruptcy and help them save face." Kerrington huffs as if to argue with him otherwise is futile. "I imagine it's tough sometimes, but ultimately, you're not the one who sank their ship. You're coming in with a lifeboat to help them."

I once thought that too, but the Greystone family, *my* family, has a reputation for being cold and heartless. We don't see people. We see debt and dollar signs.

When Mason sold BanditFX, he, Kerrington, Landon, and Gage made a lot of money. I'm the opposite of that. I buy and convert, but don't see a dime. The Greystone Family Trust does. Yes, I can pull from it whenever I'd like, but that has stopped. When Mason blew up the gala and we got out of our "arrangement", he got to live his happily ever after with no recourse. I self-sabotaged with the two men in my arms right now, and my life blew up immediately afterwards. I haven't taken a penny from the accounts since. All I have is my biweekly paycheck, which has made my current lifestyle unsustainable.

"My father is forcing me to move to Japan."

Saying the words out loud makes me feel like shit. I've just turned a wonderful afternoon into a drama fest. That seems to be all I know how to do.

But I need to talk to someone about it. I could have vented to Leah and Mason, but I don't want their pity, and I don't want to disrupt the great thing they have going. And as for talking to my best friend Grace, Mason's sister, she's going through her own shit right now and to pile on more misery isn't fair. So, her telling me Kerrington and Landon would be at Mason's this week was perfect timing.

"I leave in ten days."

They're exchanging looks again. They do that a lot. I can't imagine knowing someone well enough to read their expression and know what's in their heart. But these two do it all the time. I want a piece of that. To belong and be understood.

"For how long?" Kerrington asks.

"Until I get in line." I think I'm going to be sick. I'm pushing thirty, single, with no degree or direction in life. I just do what I'm told and will bend over backwards to make someone else proud. My life sucks. "So basically, I'm fucked. I'll be in Japan for the rest of my life."

I try to laugh it off, so it doesn't hurt so much.

"Get. In. Line." Landon acts like the concept is so foreign, he has to repeat it again and again for his mind to make it click. "You're one hell of a talented businesswoman and you've made the Greystone Foundation *huge* over the past five years. What the fuck more do your parents want from you?"

I don't have an answer for that. I just know I ruined what was left of my reputation by being with Kerrington and Landon at the club and going back to the hotel with them that night. My father called me a whore the next day and my mom stays clear of me most of the time.

"I'm sorry. *What*?" Landon shoots up from the bed.

Oops. I guess I said some of that out loud. I hadn't meant to.

"Your parents are pieces of shit. No wonder they're best friends with Mason's family."

"Landon," Kerrington chides. "They're still her family. Watch your mouth and tone."

"Fuck that!" He paces back and forth at the foot of the bed. His jaw clenches and face turns redder and redder.

Now I feel horrible.

"I'm sorry. I shouldn't have said anything." I don't know why I opened my big dumb mouth to begin with. "Can we turn back time again and just start at the part of the day where you were blowing my back out on the corner of the bed, Trick?"

He's not amused. "Don't belittle your fucking feelings or your worth, Nicole." He runs his hands angrily through his hair. "Why don't you just leave?"

"And go where?"

"Home with us!" he shouts.

"It's not that simple."

"*Yes.* It is." Now he's good and mad.

Kerrington stiffens. "Landon."

"What?" He tosses his hands up. "How are you not enraged by all this?"

"I am. But she doesn't need anger right now. She needs peace."

I think I need both. Some terrible part of me finds it nice to see Landon so angry on my behalf. No one else has ever been so enthusiastically furious over me before. But Kerr is right too. I don't want to be swept away by fury. I want peace and silence. Comfort.

"I don't understand why you won't just tell everyone to kiss your fucking ass and leave them."

My mood sours quickly. "Because I can't

just walk away from everything."

He sits on the edge of the bed and grabs my hand. "You're not walking away from everything, Nicole. You're walking *to* everything."

"Landon. Stop." Kerrington sits up. "She doesn't need this right now."

Before I can agree or disagree, Landon storms out of the bedroom. I think he's taken my heart with him because it feels awfully hollow in my chest once he's out of my sight.

"Give him some time to cool down, baby." Kerrington kisses the back of my shoulder. "He feels everything deeply. It'll take him a minute to see straight, but he'll be back, hyper and happy as ever."

I had no idea Landon was this extreme.

It makes me wonder what else I never knew about him. And how the hell do they know so much about me? Pivoting the conversation, I switch tactics. "How did you know I like spicy food?"

"I'm usually sitting across from you at dinner. And you always order something that'll make your eyes water and nose run. Glutton for punishment much?"

I laugh because he's right. "I like food that tries to kill me. Keeps life interesting."

"I remember that contest you entered with the hot wings."

"Oh yeah?" I waggle my brows at him.

"Made you boys a pretty penny that day, didn't I?"

"Fuck yeah, you did." Kerr kisses my forehead again and settles us both back in the bed. "Mason and I were both scared to death that you were pushing yourself too far in the final round. You looked like you couldn't breathe up there."

"Well, that which does not kill you, raises the bar on the Scoville scale."

"Like I said. Glutton. For. Punishment."

"Tell me about it. My pride cost me a week in the bathroom afterwards. Worth it though."

Kerrington's head tips back and a laugh so bold and lovely flies out of him. "You're a fucking menace."

Preening, I relax against him and close my eyes. "Glad you appreciate my humility."

"I appreciate everything about you, baby."

"Thank you." I curl against him a little tighter. "For being here for me."

"We aren't going anywhere, Nicole. I promise."

No. They aren't. I am. "I don't want to leave…" *you* is on the tip of my tongue, but I bite down on it.

"Shh." He straightens our covers and cuddles up with me. "That's not a problem for today, Duchess. Just relax and let me hold you."

I lay there in the arms of one man, while longing for the other to join us.

"I envy him," Kerrington says quietly.

Craning my neck to lock gazes with him, I wait for him to continue.

"Landon walks through life knowing exactly what he wants and isn't ashamed to go for it. If people have something to say, he lets it bounce right off his back. He lives every day as if it could be his last and doesn't give a shit about anything other than chasing his happiness and owning his truth."

"You don't?"

Kerrington shakes his head. "I'm trying. But… it's hard. I'm not very good at confessing my feelings or living so loudly."

"I think you live loud enough."

"Oh yeah?" He smiles at me. "How so?"

"The tension you bring is… very noticeable. The way you look at Landon." I sigh. "I would sometimes pretend catching you looking at me that way too."

"What way is that?"

"Like you'd do anything to get inside me." I swallow hard. "Like you'd kill to protect me." Okay, now I'm being overly dramatic.

"Is that so?" Kerrington tips my chin, so I have to look at him. "How am I looking at you now?"

Like I'm the only thing that exists. "Like you just came really hard and are now hungry for loaded cheese fries and a half pound burger with bacon."

Kerrington gawks at me and, even though we both know I ruined the moment, he lets it slide. "You're right."

"I knew it." Patting his chest, I get comfy again. "See? I know you really well, too. I can read you like a book."

"At least I'm a pretty book."

"Oh yeah, for sure. With all the sprayed edges and gorgeous interior artwork."

Kerr chuckles. "It's nice you think that, Duchess."

I lay on my back too, and we both end up staring at the ceiling. "I've never felt more like myself than when I'm with you guys."

He blindly reaches for my hand and holds it. "Same."

The door slams shut, signaling that Landon has left the suite, and I immediately sit up, wanting to chase him down.

"Don't worry." Kerrington pulls me back down on the bed. "He'll be back soon."

"Are you sure?"

"I can read him like a book, too." We lay in silence for a little while longer and then Kerrington pops up on his elbows and flashes me a killer smile. "Wanna give him an incentive to hurry back fast, Duchess?"

"What do you have in mind?"

Chapter 18

I've already placed an order for one of every combo deal on the menu of this burger joint and am impatiently waiting for my number to be called. So of course, I'm stewing and reflecting.

Kerrington's right. Nicole needs comfort. Not a knight in shining armor. I keep forgetting who we're dealing with here. She's got Kerr's confidence and seriousness, with my fuck it attitude sprinkled on top. It takes a lot to get Nicole to snap, but when she does, she's vicious about it.

Our girl has always taken care of herself. Until now. She's too thin, too tired, and too sad. I can't help but think if we'd hounded her harder, showed up at her door and made her let us into her life more, then we could have helped her before things got so bad. Fucking hell, I can't believe her parents would treat her so horribly and let her get this unhealthy. If she was my family, I'd take care of her the same way Kerrington and I take care of each other. Whatever I need, he'll get me and vice versa.

We're there for each other, no matter what.

So right now, I'll be there for Nicole as her support, whatever that may look like. If she needs to be fucked into next Tuesday, fine. If she needs to be spoon-fed every meal so she can have some nutrition back in her system, I'll happily do that too. And if she needs me to have a come-to-Jesus moment with her family on her behalf, I'll make them see God.

Okay. I've got this. No more getting upset on her behalf. I'll just be there to help her have happiness and fun.

We'll have one solid week of good times. Seven days of fuckery. One-hundred-sixty-eight hours of coming and laughing and snuggling and doing anything our little hearts desire.

We've got this.

"Excuse me," an elderly woman says, trying to get past me so she can fill her fountain soda cup.

"Sorry, ma'am." I sidestep out of her way when my cell buzzes in my pocket. Pulling it out, I'm a little confused at first. It's a text from Kerrington. A video clip? What the hell. He never sends videos.

Tapping play, my body locks when I see a zoomed in shot of his dick.

Oh my god.

I tuck myself into the corner by the end of the counter and swallow hard as I watch the recording.

"Put it in, baby." Kerrington's voice is low and gruff. I turn up the volume, so I don't miss anything.

Nicole reaches for his dick and wraps her slender fingers around the base before lowering her sweet body down on him.

"Oh yeah," Kerrington groans.

The camera jostles and suddenly I'm no longer breathing. When Kerr's fully seated in her pussy, they both let out a groan like it's the best motherfucking feeling in the whole wide world.

God Damnit. I'm missing out on the fun again!

"Go slow," he orders her.

Nicole glides up and down his shaft and I can see the cream she leaves behind on him. I turn the volume up even more, hoping I can hear some fun wet noises.

Kerrington rolls her over and the video jostles again. Then he aims the camera right where they're joined. Oh, hell yeah. This angle is even better. She's on her back, legs spread with his big veiny dick half inside her.

My cock is so fucking hard right now.

Kerr hands the phone to Nicole so she can get a clip of him absolutely railing her. She makes a bunch of short grunts every time he thrusts inside her tight pussy, then he pulls out and pumps his length, like the tease he is, and says, "Show Trick what's waiting for him, Duchess."

Nicole dips the camera to her exposed pussy

and plays with it, before spinning the camera around and blowing me a fucking kiss. "Hurry back, handsome."

She winks and the video ends.

I think I might just bust a nut in my fucking pants.

"Number twenty-seven!"

I start the video again because once isn't enough. Shit, ten times won't be enough.

"Number twenty-seven!"

I restart the video again, loving the noises they make together. Real talk? Watching the two people I love most in the world fuck each other is exhilarating.

"Number twenty-seven!"

"Excuse me, young man." The old woman from earlier pokes my arm, making me jump. "Is that your number?"

"Number twenty-seven!" calls out the cashier.

Huh? Shit. Wait. What number am I again?

Fumbling with my phone and receipt, I drop my damn cell with the video still playing. Screen face up. For all to see.

There's Kerrington's dick, sliding into my girl's pussy again. The volume sounds louder against the tile too.

The old woman gawks while a man to my left happily watches with a big grin.

I swiftly pick up my phone, snatch the food bags off the counter, and head to the car. Once inside, I slam the door shut and video call them.

Kerrington shows on the screen first. "I knew that would get your attention." His deep chuckle makes me melt. "You on your way back yet?"

"I can't even leave the parking lot. My dick's so hard, I'll be arrested for driving impaired."

Nicole cracks a laugh in the background, and I swear all my worries lift right off my shoulders and soar into the clouds. She takes the phone from Kerrington, flashing me a smile that's brighter than the sun.

Whatever I left the hotel suite upset about doesn't even exist anymore. All I see, all I feel, is the love I have for these two.

I flash my girl a cocky grin. "You miss me already, don't you?"

"Yes." She walks through the suite with the phone. "Are you coming home now?"

Home. Home is the two of them wherever they are. Fuck yeah, I'm coming home.

"I'm on my way," I say, already strapping in.

Her eyes light up and cheeks blush. "See you soon."

I hang up first and zoom all the way back to the hotel suite.

•••

The struggle is real. Why the hell did I order

so much food and so many fucking drinks? Juggling bags in one arm, while carrying the beverage caddy in the other, means I can't get the stupid card key out to use it on the elevator without a major balancing act.

Okay... if I can just... reach into my pocket and...

Yes! Got my wallet. Now, if only I can... alright, yes, pulling the card out with my teeth works.

Look at me being so smart.

Holding the card key in my mouth, I bend down slowly and tap it against the built-in reader. *Whack.* The button to the floor I need won't light up. *Whack, whack.* Damnit, just fucking go! *Whack-whack.* Shit! I almost spill the drinks again. Damnit, man!

WHACK!

There we go. Finally, the floor I need lights up and the elevator rises.

Phew. Made it.

I head straight for the hotel suite with my two favorite people inside. There's no way I'm going to balance all this shit again and try to unlock the door myself, so I kick it a couple times to knock on it.

Nicole answers the door and *fuuuuuuuuck.*

The bags and drink caddy fall out of my hands.

Oh hell to the motherfucking yeah, baby.

My phenomenal woman's in a collar, leash,

nipple clamps, and has red Shibari rope wrapped around each of her thighs.

"God damn." I practically prowl towards her.

"Thought you'd like an appetizer," Kerrington says from the kitchen area.

Nicole giggles, backing up with this fantastic sway to her hips.

I step over all the food and spilled drinks, slamming the door slam shut behind me. "Fuuuuck, Duchess."

"You like?" Nicole spins slowly for me to get a three-sixty view of what I'm about to devour.

"I don't like. I *love*." Snatching her hand, I jerk her towards me. "Get over here."

Her mouth meets mine with a feverish hunger that sends happy signals straight to my cock.

"I'm glad you came back."

"I'm sorry I left at all. Looks like I missed all the fun." Twirling her around, I appreciate the view again. "Fuck me sideways, woman. You look good all bound and clamped."

Her cheeks redden. "Kerr said your favorite color is red."

"My favorite color is whatever you're wearing at any given moment."

Grabbing her ass, I lift her up and she wraps her legs around my middle. We kiss hard and fast, starved for each other.

She threads her fingers through my hair, and I love how wild her eyes look right now. She's freshly fucked and still needy and I gotta say this might be my most favorite way to have her. "Get inside me, Trick."

I bite one of her clamped nipples, making her cry out. "Use your manners, Duchess."

"Please get inside me, Trick. I need you now."

And I need you always, I think, just before giving Nicole what she's begging for.

Chapter 19

Nicole

Once Landon gets me on the bed, his hands and mouth are all over me.

"You turn me into an animal, Duchess."

I bite my bottom lip, enjoying how ravenous he is for me. It's so easy to forget about life when I'm in a room with these two men.

Kerrington watches us from the doorway. There's a longing in his eyes that makes me want to beg him to join us. So why do I keep my mouth shut?

"Fucking hell, Kerr. You did amazing on these." He runs his fingers over the intricately knotted rope around my thighs. It's snug, but not uncomfortable and I feel so sexy with them on.

He buries his face between my thighs, licking and sucking on me. Jesus, he's too good at this. Already my body is hot and buzzing with arousal.

"You came inside her," Trick states, after coming up for air.

"Didn't think you'd mind." Kerrington smiles at me from the doorway, giving me a little reassurance.

"Fuuuuck, the two of you on my tongue at the same time is incredible." Landon goes back for more while I keep my gaze on Kerrington.

Shouldn't I feel like a dirty whore? I fucked one man and I'm about to do it again with another. I'm dripping. Whimpering. Tied, clamped, and spread. I probably should feel ashamed for liking this so much, but I can't find that emotion anywhere. All I feel is beautiful and wanted.

Cherished.

"I'm going to fuck you so hard." Landon tears his shirt off and starts unbuckling his pants. His eyes shutter with a dark need that makes my breath catch. I've never had a man look at me the way he does. It's intoxicating. "I'm going to come inside you, so you have both of us in there at the same time."

His words only crank my desires up ten thousand more notches.

I want them to fuck me, at the same time, in the same hole. What do I have to do to get that?

Now doesn't seem like the time to ask. I want to give Landon a little one-on-one attention like I did Kerrington. But later I'll beg for what I want most.

"Fuuuuuck," I moan, when he works his way inside me.

Kerrington prowls over to us with his hands clasped behind his back. "How does he feel,

Duchess?"

"Big." My back arches as Landon thrusts slowly in and out of me. Landon moves like a wave, surging and powerful, and he hits some kind of pleasure point deep inside me. I close my eyes, relishing every inch of him. "God, he feels so good."

Bzzzzzz.

My eyes fly open when a strong vibration hits my clit, and I gasp.

"Just relax," Landon says with a devilish grin. "Let us play."

Kerrington holds the wand to my clit while Landon fucks me harder. I ride up the bed and slam my hands on the headboard to brace myself. The ropes dig into my quivering thighs. My nipples are getting too tender with the clamps. The onslaught of so many things happening at once makes me check right out. I can't think. I can't keep up. I can't speak.

"She's gonna blow," Landon says, keeping his thrusts steady.

My lungs burn. A chill sweeps over me and my nipples fucking hurt so goddamn good. "Oh my god, oh my god, oh my—"

The orgasm strikes me like lightning, sending shocks of pleasure zooming through me until white dots dance in my vision.

My nails break when I claw the headboard, trying to find some kind of purchase so I can hold onto my sanity. The climax seems to go on forever. Until I can't feel anything. I can't see. I can't hear.

Then I fucking climax again.

It's enough to break me into pieces. My heart pounds in my chest painfully. I'm hot and cold. Floating and sinking.

Landon's mouth crushes against mine, and I realize I'm in his lap, riding him. Have I become possessed? What the fuck is happening?

"That's it, Duchess." He grips my hips and rocks me harder. "Take what you need."

The friction on my overly stimulated clit makes me want to cry, and yet I can't stop myself from rubbing harder, grinding against this man like he's my personal pleasure toy.

"Come inside me," I wheeze. "Please. I want to feel you fill me up, *Trick*."

He grabs my hair and pulls it, then kisses down my neck and sucks at my collarbone while I swirl my hips aggressively. It's the perfect combo of gentle and rough. He's so deep inside me, he's hitting my cervix, and I can't get enough. I'll never get enough.

"Come around my cock one more time and I'll give you what you want, Duchess."

"I... I don't think I can." I'm so spent, there can't be anything left to give him.

"Yes, you can, baby," Kerrington encourages from somewhere in the room. "Be our good girl and do what you're told."

"Fuuuuck," Landon growls. "She just

squeezed me so hard."

"That's it," Kerrington coaxes me. "Grind on him, Duchess. Use his big cock however you want and give us one more."

"Fuck me like a whore," Landon says against my ear.

My body tightens, and I clench around his dick again, making him groan.

Something takes over me. The power I have here is indescribable. Being able to give these two what they want is a heady fucking thing. The sex fog in my brain lifts a little and I decide to play.

Swirling, bouncing, grinding, undulating, until I get Landon to where he's shaking, I laugh and bite his earlobe.

"Fucking hell, woman." He tips me over and fucks me hard and fast. "Come for us."

"N-n-n-no."

Holy shit, he's in turbo mode.

"No?" He slows down and pinches one of my nipples, making me cry out. "Try that again, Duchess."

"N-not gonna… come… until you do…"

Landon looks over at Kerrington with a wry smile. "Oh, she's fun." Then he turns back to me and cocks his brow. "Beg me."

The brat in me comes out in full force and I flip him the bird.

Kerrington busts out in laughter while Landon grips my hips. "Big mistake, Duchess," he says, but I know he's teasing me.

Landon pulls out and turns me over. After cracking my left ass cheek with his palm, he thrusts inside me again. Then he grips my hips so hard, I know I'll have bruises.

It feels divine.

Rocking back into him, I meet every one of his thrusts, until I don't think I can hold back any longer. He's... fucking hell... he's hitting something in my body that makes me...

"Oh my god!" I scream while squirting all over the mattress.

Landon roars with his release, filling my pussy with hot cum. I collapse into the mattress, the soaked sheets not even registering as I try to catch my breath.

Someone rolls me over onto my back. *Landon.*

"You okay?"

I have no idea. "Yes?"

"Stay still for us, baby." Kerrington unties the ropes on my legs.

Landon holds my cheek and kisses me. "You did so good for us."

The praise makes me want to do it all over again immediately. But my arms and legs are al dente spaghetti noodles. I'd never be able to hold myself up for round two.

"The blood is going to rush back to your nipples. It'll hurt, but the pain won't last long. Ready?"

Nodding, I bite my bottom lip, already sad

that they're undoing all these things on me. It's like I'm being stripped of the title Duchess and getting turned back into Nicole, piece by piece.

Landon carefully unclamps my right side and the blood rushes back to my hardened nipple. I cry out from the pain, and he quickly sucks it into his mouth. The ache doesn't stop, but it's manageable.

Tears stream down my face.

Why am I crying?

Holding Landon against me, I focus on the heat of his mouth, the wetness of his tongue as he twirls it around my sore skin. When he pulls back, I let him.

"One more," he says in a soft tone. "You ready?"

"Yes."

The pain and surge of blood and suckling happens all over again, but knowing what to expect, this second time isn't as bad. My legs ache and belly cramps. I feel like I just went from soaring in the clouds to a crash landing on rocks.

I'm coming down from my high at an alarming speed.

"She's shaking," Kerrington announces, like we all can't see it.

Have I turned into a vibrator? The shakes are awful and I'm so confused. Laugh-crying, I can't grasp a single emotion to focus on. There's too many at once, jamming in my throat and rattling out of my body.

The room tips.

My vision darkens.

"I can't feel my face."

"We've got you." Landon scoops me up and places me in his lap. "You're in a sub drop, sweetheart. Kerr, get her water."

"Don't leave me."

"I'm not going anywhere, baby." Kerrington runs his hand over my hair and kisses the top of my head. "But I'm going to get some water from the fridge, and I'll be right back. Count to five for me, nice and loud."

"One…" I watch him turn. "Two…" My body won't stop shaking and I'm all wet and sticky. "Three…" He vanishes out of my sight. "F-f-four." Tears fill my eyes. "Five." Kerrington enters the room holding a bottle of water.

"Beautiful," he coos, dropping to his knees at the foot of the bed. "Look at you, being such a good girl."

His praise keeps fucking me up. I love being called a good girl as much as I love Landon telling me I'm a whore. How can I be two things at once?

"Talk to us," Kerrington says.

"Take three sips of water first," Landon orders. His arms are snug around my body, caging me in a warm, safe space.

Kerrington holds the bottle to my lips, and I do what I'm told.

"I'm so proud of you." Landon finger-combs my hair. "Can you take one more sip for us?"

Easy.

"Amazing," he says with a big smile.

All the chaos riding my system slows down. My energy is gone. Taking deep breaths, I rest my forehead on his shoulder with my eyes closed and stay in his lap until I hear running water in the bathroom.

"I want you to take a bath." Landon grips my shoulders and pushes me back so he can see my face. "Think you're up for that?"

"I'm up for anything you want me to do."

His smile takes up all the space in my heart. "Good to know."

He cradles me in his arms and carries me into the bathroom where Kerrington is diligently lighting candles. There are bubbles in the water and the sweet smell of lavender wafts in the air.

"You guys sure love your baths," I tease as Landon helps me into the tub.

"We love anything that lets us pamper the other," Kerrington says.

They both strip down and I'm momentarily stunned by their beauty. Thank God for big soaking tubs.

Kerrington slips behind me while Landon sits across from us. Our legs are all tangled and the water rises so high, it sloshes out a little. Not that any of us care.

Laying against Kerrington, I close my eyes and sigh.

We stay quiet for a long time, just basking in the sheer delight of just being.

Being together.

Being comfortable.

Being us.

"I don't want a week," I say quietly, almost hoping they don't hear my confession. And maybe they don't because neither of them speak. The silence makes my heart sink a little and I open my eyes to see Landon staring at me with a blank expression.

"How long do you want then?" he asks with an overwhelming amount of caution in his tone.

"I don't know."

Because asking for forever would be too fucking selfish. Besides, they'll tire of me sooner rather than later and kick me to the curb. If I'm the one to put an expiration date on this, at least I'll have some semblance of control over my heart break when it's over.

"What about Japan?" Kerrington says, adding more chill to the air than Landon's tone has.

Japan. I'd momentarily forgotten about that. I'm such a fool. "I don't know."

Kerrington's sigh makes me want to hide. Landon looks away, clenching his jaw.

"I'm turning into a prune," I eventually say, climbing out of the tub.

If I'm the first to go, they won't see how desperate I am to stay. Right?

Chapter 20

Kerrington

Nicole needs to be real with herself and us. If this is truly only going to be a week-long fantasy, then maybe Landon and I should pull the plug on it now. We're already in too deep with our hearts, and it's like Nicole doesn't see it at all.

"Does she really think we can't see that she loves us?" Landon asks as he dries off. "It's insulting."

"You're reaching, again, Lan." I'm not sure she loves us at all. She only needs us. We're a temporary distraction. A reprieve from her sorry ass life. I hate it.

"The only thing I'm reaching is my boiling point," Landon snaps. He storms out of the bathroom, and I follow because I'm terrified that he's going to blow up again, which isn't going to help.

Instead, Landon puts on a pair of sweatpants and heads into the kitchen.

I've already cleaned up the mess he accidentally made dropping all the fast food earlier. Most of the burgers and some of the other food was salvageable, but the soda-soaked chicken nuggets and fries were not. There's also a pile of towels where about two liters of drinks spilled all over the cream-colored rug.

That hilarious moment of watching Landon see Nicole all decked out for his pleasure, dropping everything in his hands so he could touch her, and the mess that came from it is…

Reality catching up to all of us.

First the fun. Then the hunger. Then the pleasure. And last… the aftermath and mess.

Nicole is back in her robe, standing outside on the balcony.

The sun has set.

"This burger tastes like shit," Lan tosses the rest of it in the trash.

I calmly head back to the bedroom to finish getting dressed and snag my cell from the end table. Next to mine is Nicole's. Temptation wins me over and I tap the screen to see her notifications.

There are so many, it's insane.

Just one more reminder that she's a successful and busy woman with a life waiting impatiently for her to get back to it. Meanwhile, Landon and I are in limbo with our careers.

Her screen lights up with an incoming call. The name across the screen reads *TW*. Figuring it's a work thing, I let it go to voicemail. Our girl is offline for the foreseeable future.

Plugging it into the charger, I leave her

phone in the room and head back out to a cranky Landon chugging bottled water.

"You're hangry." Pulling up the map on my cell, I search for a decent restaurant when Mason's name lights up my screen. "Mason's calling."

"Answer it."

"Hey man," I turn away from Landon to check on Nicole again.

"Hey man, my ass. Where is she?"

"Still with us." I'm getting a headache. Sinking onto the couch, I rub my forehead and sigh heavily. "Why?"

"Her parents are looking for her."

"She's a grown woman, Mason. Not a teenager with a fucking curfew."

"She's a *Greystone*," he tosses back. "She's a power piece in an expensive game."

I hate that he's comparing her to a bougie pawn. "Not anymore, she's not," I say, like I have any control here.

"Fucking Hell, Kerrington." Mason catches my drift, then. Good. "What the fuck do you plan to do with her?"

"Keep her. Take care of her. Runaway with her if we have to."

His silence makes me want to scream. As far as dropping the Hey-bestie-I've-been-in-love-with-your-ex-fiancé-for-forever bomb goes, I probably should have handled this with a little more class and respect.

Too late to take it back.

"Good," he says, shocking me. "It's about fucking time, bro."

I almost drop my phone. "What?"

"You heard me." Mason chuckles. "I was wondering when you were going to finally admit that you love her."

My heart falls between my feet. "You knew?"

"Of course, douchebag. And FYI, Landon does too, so if he's not on the same train as you, he better get on board before I kick his ass."

"He's on board," I say quickly, a smile trying to work its way across my face. "He's willing to kidnap and keep her hostage in our basement."

"You don't have a basement."

"That's what I said." Laughter bubbles out of me and relief makes me a little lightheaded. I honestly had no idea how we were going to tell Mason about Nicole. It's one thing to go out dancing for a night, but it's another to want to keep her forever with us.

"You should have said something sooner," Mason chides. "I would have supported you."

I guess that's true, but… "It wasn't right. With you two engaged. There was no way I, or Landon, would've ever touched her."

"Even though you knew I was doing everything in my power to get out of it?"

"Yeah." I lean back, running my hand down

my face. "I wasn't going to step in until I knew for sure that…"

Nicole opens the balcony door and steps back inside, her hair wind-blown and the tip of her nose bright red.

"Knew for sure that what?" Mason asks, forcing me back on track.

"Knew that it was over for good between you two."

"Christ, I would have paid you to take her. Even if she'd been my w…" He gags. "My wi—" He gags again. "Christ, I can't even say it."

"*Wife*," I say, knowing it's all an act on his end. But when I say the word, I stare at Nicole and the burning desire to make her my wife is so fucking strong, my chest hurts.

Landon slowly approaches her from behind, wraps his arms around her waist, and presses little kisses on her temple.

Aaaaand suddenly, I see our future.

"So, she's doing okay?" Mason asks, once again making me refocus on our conversation instead of the beautiful sight in front of me.

"She's getting there." I tap my leg, beckoning Nicole over to me. She leaves Landon and sits on my lap, curling into my chest and making me feel ten kinds of protective of her.

"Leah wants to go out to dinner tonight. Do you all want to join us at the Magnolia?"

I think he really just wants to see Nicole for himself. Not that he doesn't trust us, but I know

Mase well enough to catch when he's being protective, too. We hauled her out of his house like two knights with a damsel in distress, after all.

"Let me ask." I slip Nicole's hair off her shoulder and kiss her cheek. "Mason and Leah want to meet for dinner. Do you want to go?"

"Ugh, with Mason? No. With Leah? Always."

"We're a two for one, Nicole!" Mason yells into the phone. "You know all about that kind of deal, considering you're with my two best friends."

"We'll see you at eight." I hang up quickly and give Nicole all my attention.

She giggles against me, not at all flustered by Mason's commentary. She never is. The two of them give each other a hard time about everything. It's their love language. "Two for one," she repeats, shaking her head. "Wow."

"I think he just meant you can't have one without the other."

"I know," she says, her expression somber. When her eyes meet mine, we both understand that rule goes beyond Mason and Leah. It's for Landon and me, too. "I wouldn't want one without the other," she says, her cheeks flushing. "Does that make me greedy and selfish?"

Landon sits down next to us. "No. It makes you honest and true."

Backing up Lan's comment, I offer her a

reassuring smile and nod.

Nicole shakes her head and huffs. "How do you guys act like it's so easy?"

"It's not an act," I say.

"And it *is* that easy," Landon adds. He places his hand on her thigh and captures her gaze. "You get one shot at this life, Nicole. One. Do you want to spend it chasing someone else's dream and hope for a smidgeon of joy, or do you want to go for exactly what you want and be extraordinarily happy for the rest of your life?"

Her mouth opens to argue with him, but she shuts it.

"When are you going to do what makes *you* happy, Nicole?" He cups her cheek. "When are you going to finally say fuck it? Fuck anyone who doesn't want to see you live your life how you want. Fuck anything that doesn't make you happy. Fuck everything that brings you sorrow. Fuck whatever holds you back from getting what you want most. Fuck it all."

Nicole sags in my lap, her shoulders drooping. "I don't know," she says quietly.

"What *do* you know?" Landon asks. He's not getting snippy yet, but I can tell it's coming. Landon doesn't have speeds to his emotions. He's full stop, or full throttle.

Nicole blows out an exasperated breath. "I know I can't keep living like I am."

"That's a start," he says.

"I know I want more out of my life." She

turns so she can see my face, too. "I know… I love how I feel being with you."

My heart tries to inflate but can't find the courage to.

"What else?" Landon presses.

"I know I…"

"What?" we both ask at the same time.

Her cheeks turn pink, and she clams up again.

"Nicole, we're here to help." I run my hand up and down her arm. "Whatever it is you want, we'll help you get it. We want to see you happy, baby."

Her brow pinches, like she's unsure if she should believe me or not. "I don't want to be selfish."

"You don't have a selfish bone in your glorious goddamn body," Landon says. "Nicole, seriously? You are the most generous person we've ever met."

She shakes her head, refuting it, but I grip her chin, forcing her to stop. "Tell us your selfish thing." We can argue all day and night about our views on one another, but it won't fix her hangups right now. All we can do is go along with it until we hear what it is she wants most.

Then we'll make sure she gets it.

"I'll tell you in a week," she says, copping out.

"You said you wanted more than a week," I shoot back. "Did you change your mind that fast?"

"No." Nicole bites her bottom lip again. It's a nervous tick of hers. One I've never seen her do this much, and at the rate she's going, she'll eat her mouth off.

"Be selfish." Landon tips her face to his and cocks his brow. "We want you to be the most selfish creature on earth, *Duchess*."

She swallows hard and pulls away from him.

"Okay," Nicole finally whispers.

This is a small victory in a much larger battle. One, I'm scared we won't win in the end.

Chapter 21

Landon

Going out to dinner with Mason and Leah is probably exactly what we need. It'll give Nicole a chance to talk to Mase, and we all need to eat. Besides, who doesn't want a dose of Leah's good energy? That woman can turn anyone's frown upside down, so I'm hoping like Hell she'll be able to get Nicole to let go a little more. Or at least relax.

Don't get me wrong. I love fucking our girl boneless, but it's not sustainable. Wait. Don't get me wrong with that one either. I can fuck all day and night and the only one who can match my stamina is Kerrington, so she's got plenty of dick ready to go whenever she wants it. I'm just saying sex is not all there is to what we want from her. Free use is fun and all, but we want her heart, not just her body.

It's annoying that she won't open up to us all the way and tell us what's going on in her pretty little head.

Mason might be able to get it out of her, though.

"What should I wear?" Nicole asks from the bathroom doorway. I'm shaving and Kerrington's in the shower.

"Whatever you want, Duchess." She pouts and I suddenly understand that she doesn't want to pick. She just wants to be told. "Wear my Henley and pair of leggings if you've got some. You'll be in Kerrington's coat."

She perks right up and disappears with a smile on her face. There's no good reason for putting her in our clothes when she's got a fat suitcase full of her own expensive threads, but I love seeing her in our stuff. I don't need a good reason. I just fucking want it this way. Guess she's on board with that, going off the smile on her sweet face.

Kerr gets out of the shower and it's hard to focus on shaving my jawline when he looks so goddamn scrumptious. His dark hair is slicked back and his muscles contract as he dries off.

"Want to play Control?"

With the razor poised to slide down my cheek, I send Kerrington a devilish glare. "It's been a while since we did that."

His grin goes a mile wide. "Is that a yes?"

"Fuck yes, it's a yes."

He slaps my ass and walks out of the bathroom to let me finish getting ready and to prep for the game we love to play.

When I come out, albeit it, twenty minutes later, Nicole and Kerrington are in the living room and she's on his lap, kissing him.

Goddamn I love seeing these two together. "Ready?"

"Are you?" Kerrington cocks his brow at me as he slips his hand into his front pants pocket. A second later, the butt plug in my ass vibrates and I tense.

"Mmmph."

"Words, Landon. Use them."

"I'm… fuuuuck, I'm ready." Walking with this thing going off inside me is a bit of a challenge, but I manage.

"What's happening?" Nicole asks, a little concerned.

"You didn't tell her?"

Kerrington shrugs as he gets the door for us. "Thought you'd want the honor."

"Tell me what?" Nicole rests her hands on her hips at the threshold. "What are you two up to because I want in on it."

Oh, she will be. "We sometimes play this game called Control." Fucking hell, my dick's already getting hard.

The fucker's changed the setting to pulse.

"And what's that mean?"

"I have the control." Kerrington pulls out the little fob from his pocket. "And Landon has to maintain *his* control when he orgasms out in public."

Her eyes blow wide as they sail down to my crotch. "And what happens if you lose control?"

"Oh, he will. Many, many times," Kerrington says with a cocky smile. "He loves it."

"So do you." Fucking Christ, I'm going to blow just thinking about it. I'm not usually a hair trigger, and I definitely can hold my orgasms for a while, but with this incessant stimulation, and Nicole in on it, I kind of want to blow fast just to make her watch. "Do you want to play, too, Duchess?"

"I am not going to have a buzzer in my butt while sitting across the table from Mason and Leah. No way."

"That's fine. Then be the catcher," Kerrington offers.

"And what am I catching, exactly?"

I grunt, rubbing my dick through my pants because the need for release gets too strong to hold back and behave.

Her mouth drops, and she turns to Kerrington. "Whoa."

I brace against the doorjamb. Our hotel suite door is wide open, and I'm whipping my cock out already. Pumping myself, it doesn't take long before the first orgasm strikes me. "Give me your mouth, Duchess."

She doesn't hesitate to drop to her knees and suck me off while I blow my load down her throat. It's over fast. Too fast.

"Let's go." Kerrington leaves first and I'm still helping Nicole back to her feet.

"How long will you play this game?"

"For however long I can stand it." Which will be a few hours at least. My max was eleven hours, and I thought I was going to die. It would have been a glorious death, not gonna lie.

"Do I get to catch it every time you…" She makes a little explosion gesture with her hands.

"Probably not. Unless you want to crawl under the table at the restaurant with Mase and Leah there. I certainly won't stop you."

Her cheeks blaze, and she doesn't say another word. I tuck myself away and follow her out of the suite and into the elevator, my heart pounding hard in my chest.

"You good?" Kerrington asks, already checking in with me.

"Peachy."

As we hit the lobby, the motherfucker turns the setting up to a faster, steady vibration.

By the time we're halfway to the restaurant, "I'm going to come again."

The sensations are too much to fight and the urge to stroke myself and get off is not something I'll deny. Unbuckling my belt and pulling my dick out, I stroke myself and stare at Kerrington through the rearview mirror while he drives.

"Hold it," he commands.

"Can't… too… close."

"Hold. It."

As much as I want to obey, my bratty side has other plans. Flipping him the bird, I jerk off faster. "Duchess, catch it."

Nicole insisted we both sit in the backseat, and she hasn't taken her eyes off me since. My girl leans down and sucks the head of my dick until the wave of pleasure rides through me and I lean back with a sigh. "This is gonna be a long evening."

"You're a fucking hair-trigger tonight."

I'm not insulted by it. He's right. "Can you blame me? Look at our scene. Hottie in the driver's seat with the control to my ass. And the most stunning creature in the world ready to suck me off. I'm going to take full advantage of this until I'm drained dry."

Nicole giggles and swipes cum from the corner of her mouth. Instead of licking it or wiping it on something, she reaches over and offers it to Kerrington. Without missing a beat, he sucks her finger and groans.

"Yeah. I'm in so much trouble tonight." Leaning back, I press my head against the cool window, hoping it'll help ease my burn.

Once we pull up to the restaurant and hand the keys to valet, I have to stop, mid-way up the fucking steps, and take a minute. My dick's straining for attention, pinned against the waistband of my dress slacks, and my balls are drawing up tight.

A fast climax shutters through me, making my knees buckle and I whip my arm out, holding Kerrington's shoulder to keep upright. My cock jerks in my pants, pumping cum all over the fabric. My heart beats a mile a minute.

"This is so fun," Nicole whispers loudly to Kerrington.

I flip them both the middle finger, and stand on my own again. Sweat trickles down my back.

I'm wheezing.

"After you." Kerrington holds the door for me. The bastard has the nerve to smack my ass as I go past him. Reaching out, I grab Nicole's hand and squeeze it while the hostess brings us to our table. Mason and Leah aren't here yet. Thank fuck.

Kerrington changes the setting to full blast, and I jolt in my seat.

"Tell me when you're close," Nicole urges with a recklessness to her tone.

Sweat blooms across my forehead and my vision warbles. I'm already squirming, rubbing my cock through my pants. "Fucking hell, I suck at this tonight."

Kerrington leans on his elbows and stares at me with this big, evil grin. The control is in his hand, and he makes a show of clicking the setting to a fast pulse.

"Duchess." My head drops as I squeeze my eyes shut and try really fucking hard to not... lose... contr — "I'm too close."

Nicole shimmies under the table, surprising us both completely. In a flurry, she yanks on my pants and sucks the head of my dick while I spurt out whatever cum I have left. My body is going to be bone dry after this evening. I need to drink a lot of water. When my orgasm is over, she doesn't get up, though.

"Sweet Jesus, we're gonna get arrested," I whimper, holding her head, petting her hair while she sucks me off a little while longer.

"Mason's here," Kerrington announces.

Nicole pops off me so fast, she bops her head on the table, rattling the silverware and wine glasses. While she scrambles back up into her seat, I duck away so she can't see me laugh.

This is way more fun with her joining in on the game.

"Hi!" Leah waves as she hurries over to us. We all get out of our seats to hug her, and she makes her rounds, landing next to Nicole at the table while Mason sits next to me.

"Switch," Kerrington says automatically to him.

"Aw fuck." Mason knows we play these games sometimes. He's even more into voyeurism and exhibitionism than we are. No shame in our games.

Kerrington puts his hand on my thigh once he sits next to me and we're all cuddled up in the booth together, looking out at the bar area.

The server arrives with a platter of freshly sliced citrus for our waters and takes our cocktail orders. My ass buzzes at a new setting, and I'm confused. What the —

Kerrington's not holding the remote

anymore. He's gripping his ice water with one hand, the other is resting on my thigh.

The setting changes again, making me jump a little.

Kerr squeezes my leg reassuringly, aaaaand my gaze swings to Nicole. She's got this beautifully wicked smile, half hidden behind her glass of water that's got two lemon slices floating in it. She winks and the setting changes again.

My dick's too hard for this setup. I'm going to lose control too quickly, and I've got to figure out my game plan because sitting directly across from me is Mason, watching Nicole with concern. Because of course he's worried about her. She showed up at his house, needing help, and now she's—

I blindly grip Kerrington's hand and squeeze it so hard, I think I might break it. My orgasm has my vision going white for a few seconds and beads of sweat drip down my temples.

"So how is the Brazen Bunny going?" Kerrington asks Leah and Mason while simultaneously handing me his glass of water.

I've already drank all mine.

I chug his glass in four gulps.

"I've got so many sponsors already," Leah announces with delight. "And Mase has been working on the techy stuff day and night. Were you able to finesse the payment system idea for us, Lan?"

"Of course," I say, wiping my sweaty brow. My dick's flaccid, for once, and I pray it stays that way through the main course. "I'll show you what we've got in a day or two. I'm still working on a few of the…mmph… the kinks."

Shooting Nicole dagger eyes, I swear my heart rate kicks into stroke territory as the need to touch myself takes over and I can't do anything but grin and bear it. Dinner takes forever. By the grace of all things unholy, I keep some control. I've only orgasmed two more times and with nothing left in my balls, my pants are barely soaked.

"Good boy," Kerrington growls against my ear as he pretends to reach over for the salt. "You look amazing all spent and relaxed."

Mason, Leah, and Nicole are rattling off about something I'm too spaced out to keep up with. Our girl changed the setting just before dessert, and I've been coasting through a long, weak climax that's lasted several minutes.

"You still doing okay?" Kerrington whispers casually in my ear.

I nod, taking another sip of water.

"Need a break?"

I shake my head and clench my teeth. My control improves the more I come, anyway. My body numbs out once subspace and exhaustion kicks in.

Doesn't mean I don't have the shakes, though. It feels good.

Nicole secretly rests her hand on my other thigh, and I love having them both touch me at the same time.

Our gazes all swerve to the approaching server. "Is there anything else I can get you?"

"Just the check, to me, please," Mason replies.

Nicole surprises me by turning my head towards her and kissing me. The gesture comes out of nowhere and sends me soaring through the roof. A kiss is such a powerful thing sometimes, and in the state I'm in, the endorphins buzzing through my system intensify the tenderness of her touch.

"Wow," Leah says with her chin resting on her hand. "You three are so cute together."

Nicole clears her throat and takes a sip of her wine. "Who says we're together?"

"You're not?" Leah counters. "Because Lan's been doing a shit job of holding himself together all night, and Kerrington's watched the two of you like a hawk. And whatever you've got in your hand makes a sweet little clicky sound, so someone's got something happening somewhere."

Mason buries his head in his hands. "Nicole."

She drops the remote in her lap and acts all innocent. "What?"

Leah bursts into laughter. "Poor Landon."

"Don't feel bad for him," Mason huffs.

"Knowing him, he asked for it."

"I swear I didn't," I say, giving up trying to hide my exhaustion. "Jesus, I need more water. And a nap. And a shower."

Our server returns with the check, and Mason swiftly pays the bill. I think the best part of my friendships is the fact that no one ever shames me for what I like and how I like it. Mason and Leah have never played with Kerrington and I, but they support us in every way, which makes spontaneous scenes like this much more fun.

I love them.

Just as we're about to head out, Mason stops Nicole. "I need to talk with you."

Her brow furrows. "Okay. Let's go to the bar."

They leave Leah with us, and we make our way to the valet.

"Is she going to be okay?" Leah asks. "Mason's worried sick about her, and after you two hauled her out the other day, I've gotta say, seeing her this way with the two of you is nice."

"We're taking good care of her," Kerrington promises.

She gives him a hug and drops her tone. "Take care of *each other*."

"We are," I assure her. "And if we have it our way, Nicole's not going back to New York."

Leah's eyebrows rise to her hairline. "Really?"

"Really," Kerrington nods. "She's ours. We

just need her to fucking get on board with that."

"And if she doesn't?"

I shrug and stuff my hands in my pockets. "Then we're buying a house with a basement and chaining her to the radiator down there."

Leah tips her head back and cackle laughs.

Chapter 22

Nicole

Mason steers me over to the far side of the bar, getting right to business. "I hate to shit all over our nice night, but your parents have been looking for you."

My mood sours immediately. "Why are they calling *you*?" They shouldn't even know that I'm here, damnit.

"Grace must have told them you were coming."

"Ugh! Why is she snitching like that?"

"She cares about you."

My heart drops because he's right. Grace and I have been best friends for forever, and that I haven't checked in with her or told her about my struggles—because I know she's going through her own right now—makes me feel like a shithead. I should call her soon.

"What did you tell my parents?"

"That you're here for a week at the spa."

I roll my eyes because that's not going to fly. No spa in this town is bougie enough for my parents to buy that bullshit. Still, I appreciate the effort. Mason didn't have to lie like that for me. "Thank you."

"Just talk to them, Nicole."

"They don't ever listen. And after the whole gala debacle, they've been working me nonstop. I swear I'm going to lose my mind if I have to go back." Which I will soon, and I'm terrified of what my mental state will turn into when that happens. Tears prick my eyes and I'm not about to ruin a good makeup night with some saltwater leaking out of my face. Fuck that.

"You can't blame them for being worried. You should have just said you were going away for a week. Mini vacay with Grace or something. Ghosting them, and your meetings, isn't like you at all."

"Well, maybe it's exactly like me and they just don't know who I am!" I yell.

Mason glowers like he wants to either chastise me again or hug me. He better not do either. "You don't get it, Mase."

"The fuck I don't. It's why I got out."

"Exactly," I snarl. "*You got out*. I'm still fucking stuck." I slump on my stool and glare at the bar top. "I'm never going to escape, am I?"

"You can if you'd let me help you."

"I'm not a charity case."

For years I've tried to figure out a lucrative business that I can run on my own and make bank with. Just like Mason did. But all my ideas suck and honestly, I'm not cut out for it. Being a career-woman is not in my blood. And that fucking shames me the most. I came from a line of powerful millionaires, and I have neither the sense nor the desire to do what it would take to run my own company that my family would inevitably get their teeth and claws into.

Any business venture I come up with requires a boatload of start up cash. Money I don't have that's not connected to a trust fund. Money that I refuse to ask for because even getting investors or loans would mean owing someone that they'd want to take from my parents, not me. And if my parents get involved, the Greystone Trust will, too. So, I'm fucked.

To make it worse, that's not even my most crucial issue. The stress of my family isn't the only worry I'm dealing with. There's something much worse riding my tail that no one knows about, and I plan to keep it that way.

"What about Landon and Kerrington?"

Mason's question hits me like a bat to the head. "What about them?"

When he doesn't answer, I slowly turn to look at him, but his expression is too guarded for me to read.

"They're my best friends, Nicole."

"I know that."

"They're not your fucktoys."

"Says who?" I push back, and immediately feel bad about it. Exhaling, I slouch again. "I know they're not, Mase."

"Do you love them?"

I can't have this conversation with him, here in this stupid bar, with the rest of our party waiting for us outside. I don't want to have it at all.

"Answer me, Nicole."

My instinct is to go on the defense and be a brat and tell him to kiss my ass. But Mason's being sincere, and this conversation needs to be had. I haven't been able to discuss it with anyone else, including Grace, and I've got to get it off my chest before it crushes me to death.

"I need a drink first."

So much for having balls, right? I'm stalling and can't help it. Once I say this, I won't be able to take it back and Mason, the bane of my existence, will know my deepest secret. Well, one of them at least.

He flags the bartender down and orders two shots of top-shelf bourbon. Neither of us say a word until the glasses are set in front of us. He silently slides mine over and we both down our drinks.

"I'm in love with both of them." There. I said it. Does he think less of me now? Is he going to laugh? Get mad? Tell them before I do?

Looking smug, he tips his head to the bartender. "Another."

Bourbon pours into our glasses, and I recognize the label. Mason's taste in friends, women, and bourbon are impeccable. I sometimes wonder if I could have stomached marrying him. The answer is absolutely fucking not. He's got a big heart and all, but no. Just *no*. I can't see myself in a relationship where my husband and I are merely roommates in a mansion and have to fake being perfectly in love in front of people.

But isn't that what I've always done? Faked it?

I fake my happiness all the fucking time. Act braver than I am. Pretend to be something I'm not.

Gripping the fresh glass, I down it before I cry. The bourbon burns my throat and gut. I think I might throw it up.

"Don't say anything," I say quietly, not having the courage to look him in the eyes. "Please."

Mason's tone is sharp. "Nicole."

"I want to tell them myself. It can't come from you or anyone else. I just don't want to tell them yet." The whiskey's gone straight to my head, making me feel loopy. "I don't know what to do." Turning, I finally let him see how raw and scared I am.

His face falls. "Christ." Resting his elbows on the bar, he scrubs his face with both hands. "Want my advice or not?"

"Sure."

"Walk away."

• • •

When we get outside, I'm feeling so buzzed that I can't quite gauge my footing on the steps and nearly slip. Mason catches me. "Since when did you become such a lightweight?" he teases.

"Ugh." I smack his arm, even though a smile curls on my lips. "Shut up."

Kerrington's waiting for us by my car. He looks concerned. "Everything okay?"

"All good." Mason unceremoniously hands me over like I'm a sack of recycling that needs to be taken out. "You guys want to come over tomorrow?"

Kerrington glances at Landon, who's in the passenger seat. "Mmm. Give us a day to recover, then we'll be over." He opens the backseat for me. "Is that okay with you, Duchess?"

I nod, too caught up in my head to say much else.

Kerrington shuts the door, and I can't hear what the two of them are talking about because Landon's got the music turned up. He's relaxed in the passenger seat with a lazy smile on his face, as if he doesn't have a care in the world.

"How you feeling, Duchess?"

"Shouldn't I be asking you that?" Focusing on him feels better than worrying about my troubles. "You look exhausted."

"I am." He squirms a little. "But it's nice. I've been cruising in subspace for a while now.

I'm gonna sleep like a baby."

I love that for him.

Kerrington gets in the car and checks on both of us before hitting the road. The ride home is quiet. I fall back into my thoughts and the conversation Mason and I just had. Tears prick my eyes again, but I fight them for all I'm worth. I don't want Kerr or Lan to see me upset. They'll ask questions I'm not ready to answer yet.

My heart is already breaking as it is and when they find out my biggest secret, I'm fucking doomed.

Kerrington helps Landon into the hotel. Jeez, I guess having that many forced orgasms can really take it out of you. I wouldn't know. But going off how I collapsed earlier with just a couple of hard climaxes, I can only imagine what Landon's body must feel like.

"Almost there," Kerr says to him in a soothing voice. "You did so good for us tonight."

Landon offers another smile, his eyes at half mast, as he faces Kerrington and kisses him. They worship each other slowly. Thoughtfully.

"Fuck me?" Landon asks with a hopeful cadence.

"You're not too sore?"

Lan shakes his head. "No. I'm perfect."

Kerrington kisses him again and then crooks his finger, beckoning me to join them.

Funny, whenever they are together, I never feel like the third wheel. It's like I've been part of… whatever they are… and always have been. We're too comfortable for three people who haven't spent a lot of time together.

Too comfortable around each other for me to keep holding this last secret.

Kerrington removes Landon's clothes first and lays him back on the bed. Then he carefully pulls out the plug, making Landon grunt with relief.

"So. Fucking. Pretty." Kerr kisses him again. "You've been such a good boy tonight."

"Mmmph."

My mouth waters as Kerrington strips down and gets prepped.

Landon looks over at me and smiles. "Sit on your throne, Duchess."

I don't even know what that means.

"Strip and sit on his face," Kerrington explains. "He deserves a reward for his excellent behavior this evening."

My hands shake as I do what I'm told, peeling layers of clothing off my aching body and climbing onto the bed. "Which way?"

"Face me," Kerr demands. "I want to look in your eyes while I fuck him."

Before obeying, I kiss Landon, double checking to make sure he's up for this.

"You taste like expensive bourbon and heaven."

That makes me giggle, lightening my mood. "How can you tell it was expensive?"

"Baby, I'm too bougie to not know the difference between a three-dollar shot and a hundred-dollar one." He flashes me a big smile and crooks his finger at me. "Saddle up, sweetheart. I skipped dessert in the restaurant, knowing you'd serve me a better one."

How can he make the raunchiest things so sweet?

Climbing up on his face, I hover.

"Nope." Landon hooks his arms around me. "*Sit*." With that, he forces my full weight onto his face.

Kerrington's lubed up and already spreading Landon's thighs, hiking them up. "Hold him for me."

My palms sweat as I grip Landon's knees and spread him wide. His tongue is already doing a deep dive into my pussy and the bourbon's still flowing through my system.

I groan, watching Kerrington push himself inside Landon. The way his dick slides. The way his dark hair falls into his eyes when he looks down to watch it. The way his abs bunch and flex as he slowly moves in and out.

Landon moans against me, tickling a little.

Kerrington catches my glance and holds it. The tendons in his neck tighten. His eyes harden. Jaw clenches. Then he pushes all the way in, burying himself balls deep. Abs flexing, he picks up speed, until he has both Landon and I rocking from his thrusts.

I've never been on a better ride.

Kerrington leans forward and grabs the back of my head. Our mouths fuse and it's like we're one. All three of us are one entity. One heart. One soul.

One moment that will last me a lifetime.

My eyes sting from the tears I've yet to unleash. My body sings. Everything funnels into this heady, distilled heartbeat with a pounding rhythm that rattles my bones.

Kerrington pulls back from me. Landon squeezes my hips, forcing me to ride his face harder. His thighs tense. His dick is hardening again. I feel an impending orgasm barreling down on me. Tipping my head back, I close my eyes, riding the wave.

And I scream for all I'm worth. It's not just with my pleasure. It's with my whole fucking body. My pain and regret. My fear and resentment. My hunger and hope.

Kerrington's speed quickens until he's slamming into Landon.

I lift off, terrified I'm suffocating him.

Landon sucks in a rugged breath, his back arching, and he takes what Kerrington's giving him.

Kerr roars with his release, and it's fucking glorious. The man who is so put together, so perfectly stoic and calm, unravels on top of the man who holds his heart. Wanting to know what that tastes like, I crawl forward and kiss

Kerrington while he still pumps his come into Landon. His groans turn to whimpers. Then he pulls out and away from us both.

"Fucking hell, that was amazing." Landon sits up, catching his breath.

They kiss again, and Kerrington looks concerned. "You sure you're okay? I was really rough that time."

"Couldn't be better." Landon tries to climb out of the bed, but his legs give out. "Shit."

"We've got you," Kerr says, quickly grabbing him.

We've got you.

We.

And yes, we do. I'm already holding Landon's right arm while Kerr takes the other. We escort him into the shower, and I make up an excuse about being thirsty so I can leave them alone for a minute.

We've got you.

Three simple words.

We've got you.

Such a comfort.

Feeling too vulnerable, I tear the sheet off the bed and wrap myself in it, then head to the kitchen to get each of us some water. I feel hungover. My stomach and head hurt. I think I have heartburn.

The conversation I had with Mason plays on repeat in my brain…

"Want my advice?"

"Sure."

"Walk away."

My body locks as my heart slips out of me and splatters on the polished floor. "What?"

"Walk away, Nicole. Leave everything behind and follow your heart. Wherever it leads you, that's where you belong."

The fact that I thought he was telling me to walk away from Kerrington and Landon, and the visceral reaction my instincts had to it, is a wake-up call.

"I don't think I know how."

To walk away from my entire life would be easy. But to walk away from my family too? I don't think I have the courage. I love my parents. Whether or not I'm good enough for them, I still love them. I still want them in my life. The idea of them not supporting me and my choices guts me as much as the thought of cutting them out of my life does.

But they've never supported me the way I've needed, so why do I care so much? Besides, they'll never accept me having two men in my life.

"What if it's fleeting?" I ask, letting him see the raw fear I'm clinging to. "What if I'm just a phase for them, Mason?"

I'll have given up my whole world and they'll only use me up and spit me out when I'm too boring, too annoying, or too frustrating to deal with.

"Does it feel like it's a phase?" He cocks his brow at me.

"It feels like it's too soon for this conversation."

Mason does this little side nod thing that tells me

he might just agree. "What if I told you they've been in love with you since college?"

That's impossible. I was horrible back in those days. Completely unlovable. "I'd say you're reaching, and that's unhelpful."

"I'm telling you the truth." He deadpans me. "They never touched you because of me. I'm no longer an issue, so they grabbed you the first chance they could."

At the gala.

My mind reels thinking about that night again. We were so perfect. So right. So happy. I'd gaslighted myself so many times into believing that it was just a wild night where we could each be someone we're not. It was a fantasy. A rebellious act that wasn't meant to last.

But that's not the truth.

We were ourselves. We were real. And we were so. Fucking. Happy.

"Walk away," Mason says again. "You won't regret it, Nicole."

Kerrington's laugh brings me out of my head. Filling three glasses with ice water, I tuck them against my chest and carry them into the bedroom. Landon's pulling sweatpants on and Kerrington's drying off his hair.

My heart bubbles with joy at seeing them like this.

"I have water." Hurrying to Landon first, he takes two of the glasses and hands one to Kerrington. "Thank you, sweetheart." He kisses my forehead, making me feel precious, and I almost spill the beans and tell them everything I've been holding back.

But my cell phone suddenly rings and I shut down automatically when I see the number.

TW.

My blood runs cold.

"Are you going to answer it?" Landon asks, innocently.

Not a chance.

Chapter 23

Kerrington

Something's up with Nicole. When walking out of the restaurant with Mason, she looked terrified, and that same expression is back on her face now.

TW lights up her phone screen. My protective instincts go ballistic and without saying a word, I pick up her cell from the charging station.

She's on me so fast, I drop the damn thing, and it falls under the bed.

"Don't," she snarls.

My hackles rise. She's hiding something big from us. This TW person has called her before. "Who is that, Nicole?"

She glowers at me.

My gaze narrows. "What don't you want us to know?"

It's like she's turned into a rabid animal — all teeth and confusion and rage. "It's none of your business."

Landon edges closer to us like he's afraid of getting bit. "You *are* our business."

Nicole shakes her head and drops to her knees, frantically searching for the phone that's ringing again. Before I can stop her, she runs out of the room, rips open the balcony door and throws the goddamn thing over the railing.

What. The. Fuck.

Breathing heavily, she backs up, running smack into Landon, and he wraps his arms around her, whispering calming words I can't hear because my pulse is swishing in my ears.

Tossing a phone twenty-seven floors down is a little too dramatic, even for Nicole. What the fuck is going on?

I storm over to the two of them, but Landon holds his hand out, silently stopping me. We look at each other, and he shakes his head, telling me to back off because now isn't the time to push for answers.

But if not now, then when? All we do is hold off. Stall out. Wait, wait, wait. Nothing gets accomplished this way and I fucking hate it.

"No." I make my way over to them. "I've waited long enough, Landon. This is bullshit."

"She's upset."

"Coddling her will not help." I get he wants to keep her safe and all, but that can be done without shying away from the hard truths Nicole has got to face. And so must we. "We can't help you if we don't know what's going on."

Nicole shoves away from us and crosses her arms. The sheet she'd been wrapped in is long gone. She lost it when she went diving under the bed for her phone.

"Who was calling you?" My mind races through possibilities. "Who is TW?" Is it a new fiancé? If so, I think I might commit murder. I almost lost her to Mason. I'm not about to give her away to some shmuck in a Seersucker suit her parents approve of because his last name is famous, and his bank account is fat. Fuck that. Now I'm furious. *Who was it, Nicole?*"

"No one you need to worry about," she snaps back.

Covering her breasts and pussy with her hands, she backs away from us.

"Jesus Christ." Landon hurries into the bedroom and brings out the comforter to drape around her. "Sit down. Both of you."

I don't budge, and neither does Nicole.

I've always been in love with her stubborn side. Right now, however, it's pissing me the fuck off. "Sit."

"*You* sit."

"Brat."

She flips me the bird.

Fuck me running, but her spicy behavior makes blood rush to my cock. If she wants to play hardball, I'm totally down for that. "If you don't sit now, I'll make it so you can't sit later."

She rolls her eyes and doesn't budge.

"Fine. Have it your way." It takes me three seconds to reach her. I yank her blanket off and sling her over my shoulder.

"What are you—"

Smack! I spank her so hard, my palm stings. "You want to be a brat? Fine, I'll treat you like one." I slap her ass again.

"Kerrington!" she cries out, but doesn't fight me. If anything, she drapes more over my shoulder. My girl doesn't even try to block me with her hand.

"Who was calling you?"

She doesn't speak, so I spank her three more times in quick succession.

Nicole groans and I can smell her fucking arousal with her cunt this close to my face.

I drop her, not so sweetly, onto the couch. "Landon, bring me everything we bought."

"Uh."

"Do it." I haven't taken my eyes off hers. That fire burning inside her has consumed me. If she didn't want me to have fun like this, she'd open that sweet mouth of hers and say so. "What's your safe word, Duchess?"

"Teapot."

"Fuuuuuck." Landon sets all our products on the table and even shoves the sex bench closer. "Girl, you're in for it now."

Nicole arches her brow, challenging me.

This is *not* going to go how she thinks it will.

I grab the spreader bar first. "Who was it?"

"None of your business."

Click, click. I lock her ankles in place and

stretch the bar until she's spread wide.

"What did you and Mason discuss at the bar?"

She licks her lips, her gaze finally sliding off mine and onto the blindfold I'm now holding. "Not. Your. Business."

I slip it over her head and cover her eyes.

"What are you still hiding from us?"

She bites her lip and… for a fleeting moment, I almost think she's about to give us something. I hold my breath. Landon leans forward from the seat he's enjoying the show in.

Then she clams up and flips me the bird.

Brat.

Leaning forward, I suck her finger into my mouth, surprising her. "Do I have to fuck these answers out of you, Duchess?"

"You can certainly try." Her lips curl into a wicked grin. "But I'm not easy to break."

"Wanna bet?" Grabbing one last thing, I haul her over my shoulder again and carry her out onto the balcony.

Then I handcuff her to the railing.

It's freezing out here, the crisp air making her nipples harden instantly. Goosebumps ripple down her sweet body, and she shivers.

"I could leave you like this all night," I threaten.

"You won't."

She's right, but making the empty threat and having her call my bluff gives me a little relief. Sometimes I fear she thinks I'm a dick because I'm not good at expressing my emotions with words. Clearly.

I'm good at fucking them out, though.

Bending her over, I keep one hand around her waist, so she feels secure. She's not in danger of falling over the railing, but I'm sure it seems that way, given that she's blindfolded and immobilized.

"I'm going to ask you again…"

"Don't waste your breath," she says before I can finish my sentence.

I smack her ass three times for the disrespect. "Bad girl." Sinking two fingers into her pussy, I'm not surprised to find her already soaked. I pull out and stuff them into her mouth. "Suck, baby."

She wraps her lips around my digits and follows orders like a good girl.

Landon holds out a paddle for me and winks.

"Did you like forcing those orgasms on Trick earlier?"

Our girl perks up a bit. "Yes." She answers with a hint of suspicion, which I like.

Landon leans in and growls in her ear, "What comes around, goes around, Duchess."

I shove two fingers in her pussy again, moving them fast and hard as I crack down on her ass with the smooth side of the paddle.

She cries out and grips the railing she's

chained to.

Good. She'll need to hold on for this ride.

I crack her ass again, then flip the paddle over to rub and soothe her red skin with the soft side.

"Oh my god," she groans.

Switching positions, I brace my ass against the railing and stand between her and the iron bars. Reaching between her thighs again, I sink my fingers into her cunt and mercilessly hit her G-spot while alternating the sides of the paddle.

Pain. Pleasure. Pain. Pleasure.

Pain-pleasure-pain-pleasure-pain.

She screams and shakes with her orgasm. Our pretty Duchess squirts all over herself, me, and the balcony. It drips off the goddamn railing. White clouds burst from her mouth as she sucks in ragged breaths.

I don't relent.

If anything, I double down.

Pain. Pleasure. Pain. Pleasure.

This goes on and on until she orgasms four more times.

Wrung out, she drapes over the railing with the spreader bar keeping her gaping for us. She's perfection in the moonlight.

"You're so beautiful," I rasp against her ear.

Whimpering, she leans against me and doesn't respond.

"Want to tap out yet?"

"N-no." Sweat dampens her skin, even

though it must be thirty degrees out here.

"Want to tell us who that phone call was now?"

"Definitely not."

"Suite yourself." I shove a dildo into her next. One in her pussy, and a smaller, lubed one up her ass.

Landon's doing a great job at reading my mind, and the scene, offering me toy after toy to pleasure her with.

"You want to be fucked by both of us, don't you?"

"More than anything," she whimpers.

"Think you can take two cocks in this sopping pussy, Duchess?" I stuff a finger inside her, along with the dildo, just to see if she's able to take that much.

She does with no trouble.

Our girl is primed and ready.

Too bad she hasn't earned that pleasure reward yet.

Collar, I mouth to Landon. He retrieves that and the leash within seconds. When I lock it in place around her throat, she groans again.

"Our Duchess likes being punished," Landon teases.

"She must, since she does everything in her power to get in trouble."

Nicole groans again and grips the railing, bracing for whatever I might do next.

"I want inside this ass," I warn, nipping her

shoulder. "You going to let me in, baby?"

"Yes."

"Yes, what?"

"Yes, Daddy."

Fuuuuuck. I've never been a Daddy before, and I gotta say I'm a little mad it's taken me this long to discover how much I like it. Grabbing the lube from Landon, I lather a healthy amount onto my dick, then drizzle some into her ass crack. Playing with her hole, I rim and tease, just for fun, before pressing against it with the head of my throbbing cock.

"Stay relaxed," I coach her. "And just push out a little for me."

"I know what to do," she snips impatiently.

That earns her another spank. I'm just trying to keep her safe. There's no need for the back talk. When I press against her again, however, she does what I tell her.

"That's it." My dick is much bigger than the little dildo we just played with. It's going to take encouragement and patience to get inside her this way. "You're doing so good for me, Duchess."

I ease into her nice and slow, a little at a time, until I bottom the fuck out.

Goddamn, she's tight.

And warm.

And perfectly made for us.

Rocking into her slowly, I give her time to adjust. "That's a good girl."

She whimpers, her fingers bright white

from how hard she's gripping the railing. "Harder."

I look over at Landon, a little surprised. He shrugs and goes back to watching where we're joined.

I thrust into her a little more forcefully. She yelps and loses her footing, but catches herself. "Again."

I give our Duchess exactly what she wants, how she wants it.

If only she could understand we'd be this way in every aspect of our lives together, if she'd only give us a fucking chance.

Our bodies slap together. Soon, I'm sweating too.

She comes two more times, and I love the sounds she makes and the way her cunt is dripping. It's a fucking swollen mess. Her ass is red. Her body won't stop shaking.

"More!" she cries out.

I fuck her like an animal until we're both grunting, feral, mindless creatures on the balcony. Yanking the leash, I choke her just enough to make her come again.

I've never met a woman who sets fire to my blood the way she can.

"I fucking love you." I growl, railing her harder. "Do. You. Hear. Me." Each thrust punctuates my words. "I..." *Slam.* "Fucking." *Slam.* "Love." *Slam.* "You."

Nicole screams out my name and squirts all

over herself again.

Just like earlier with Landon, I'm in awe that she has any fluids left at this point.

I fuck her harder. Mercilessly. I spank, bite, pinch, and claw at her. I love that she doesn't use her safe word. I love that she's screaming my name.

My climax finally breaks loose and surges through me in a raging fire. I roar with my release like a man free-falling straight into hell.

I've never felt so free in my life.

When I finally pull out, Nicole collapses in a heap of cum, sweat, and tears.

Landon and I make quick work of uncuffing her, and she rips the blindfold off just as I scoop her into my arms and carry her back inside.

"We've got you," I say, taking her into the bathroom.

She looks entirely too pale and flushed. Fuck, I think I overdid it.

Her ass is cherry red. Her cheeks and the tip of her nose are too. Her bright and shiny eyes lock on me, and I feel every kind of way about it.

Setting her on her feet so I can get a towel for her backfires. My girl folds like a lawn chair. "Kerrington."

Holding her against me to keep her upright, I let Landon set things up for us. Aftercare is paramount.

"We've got you," I say again, trying to soothe her.

"Stop saying that," she whines, half-heartedly smacking my biceps.

"But we *do* have you, Nicole," Landon argues.

She starts crying, and I have no idea why. Is she hurt? Is it a sub drop? Is it whoever that phone call was from?

Is it us?

Nicole sobs into my chest, making it impossible to tear away from her, even to start a bath or get a bottle of water, or take in a full breath.

I suddenly realize breathing is inconsequential when she's in my arms like this.

Maybe I'm a little fucked up, but I like breaking things just to put them back together. I like being needed in a way that's special. I like that she takes what I give her and begs for more, even if it hurts.

I love giving pain with pleasure.

I hurt her.

I want to hurt her more.

I'm a monster.

The old Kerrington shows up in my head. The one who walked in shame for indulging in my kinks until Landon showed me how to hurt without breaking. How to take without destroying.

I'm a piece of shit. I should have never gone that far. I shouldn't have liked it so much.

She's going to hate me for this in the morning.

I know these thoughts are my guilt and insecurities coming out to play. And I know how to deal with my demons now. Reaching blinding for Landon, I use him like a lifeline.

"I'm in a Dom drop," I say, but my voice sounds far away.

"It's okay," Landon says, getting me down on the floor with Nicole. "I've got you both."

Chapter 24

Landon

Well ain't this some shit.

It's been forever and a day since Kerrington has gone hard enough to put himself in this position. It's not that he's extreme with his sadism, but the man does love to break things. He's been on a short leash for a long time with me, because he knows I don't like pain, but I'm kind of proud of him for pushing his boundaries with our girl. At least he has someone to play with that side of him now.

Too bad shit's gone haywire again.

She's hiding something big from us. Big enough to make them both challenge each other. And look, I love me some top-tier bratty behavior, but I think she really pushed him over the edge this time. I can't remember the last time Kerr had a fucking Dom drop. It took a crazy amount of aftercare to get his head on straight, and a lot of convincing on Nicole's part to show she was not only okay, but loved what they did out there.

I know I fucking did.

But there's still a huge elephant in the room

with us. I want to know who this TW person is as much as Kerrington, damnit. Her behavior leads me to believe they're a threat, not a mutual. The possibility sets my teeth on edge.

Once they were cleaned up and tucked into bed, I went in search of her phone while they crashed. It's currently three in the morning. The entire world is fast asleep. All but me and the busted cell phone I retrieved from outside.

It's completely shattered and unsavable, potentially taking Nicole's secrets to its grave.

"What are you doing?" Kerrington asks in a groggy, raspy voice.

His eyes are a little swollen and his hair is a mess. Shirtless, he crosses his arms and walks over to me.

"How do you feel?" I kiss him gently, just a peck, to comfort him.

"Amazing and awful at the same time."

Kerrington's never fully embraced his sadistic side. He fucks me how I like, not how he likes. His view of himself has always been a little skewed. The man has no clue how incredible he is. He just looks at his kinky side as monstrous, I think. Such a shame.

The fact that Nicole has welts on her ass and thighs, scratch marks down her back, and teeth indents on her shoulders probably doesn't help his guilt trip. It's a helluva sight.

A stunning one, if you ask me.

"You know she loved it, right?" We talked

about it earlier while I was cleaning them both up, and the discussion went on and on until Nicole crashed and Kerrington held her tight, as if she was his lifeline, and then he too fell asleep. I'm pretty sure he partially clung to her to make sure she didn't run away from him in the middle of the night.

Not that I thought for one second she would.

"I'm scared she's going to regret this in the morning," Kerrington confesses.

"Impossible."

"I was an animal."

"Not hardly. She fucking loved it. Nicole likes it rough, Kerr."

Kerrington scrubs his face. "She's not going to be able to sit for a week with how much I spanked her."

The pain in his voice tears my heart in half.

"She has a safe word and knows how to use it."

"As her Dom, I should have stopped at a certain point."

"No, as her Dom, you should have read her like you did, listen to her cues, and act accordingly, which is exactly what you did." I grip his shoulder and squeeze until he looks at me. "She's a big girl. She loved it. Maybe she likes it rougher than you. Ever think of that?"

"That's my biggest concern," he says carefully. "How much more could I have done?"

"Guess we'll find out soon enough."

Kerrington steps away from me, shaking his head. "I'm not going to unleash that part of me ever again, Landon. Not after…"

My heart sinks. He's referring to the time he went all in with me, and I couldn't take it. I safe worded out and needed three full days to recover before I let him touch me again. It's not that he did anything wrong, because I loved it all. But the intensity was too much. Kerrington likes to push boundaries, specifically his own, and he doesn't trust himself to not lose control completely.

I've told him time and time again that the responsibility isn't solely on his shoulders. His partner or partners have control over this, too. I safe worded. We discussed what worked and what didn't. What we both loved and didn't like. Then we adjusted accordingly. But he never went full throttle on me again.

It's left a strange black mark on my heart because I want to give him everything he needs. But that's not always possible and I've had to come to terms with it. Besides, he can't give me everything I need either, so in that regard, we're even.

It can't be a coincidence that Nicole fills our voids. She's able to take Kerrington's intensity, and she also fills the sub role for me, which Kerrington could never.

"Can you fix it?" He asks, breaking our silence.

"No." We both stare at the busted cell phone, feeling inadequate for being tech tycoons. It's not every day I come across a device or program I can't get into. If it had just busted, that would be easy. But oh no, several cars ran it over before I found it in the middle of the street, crushed. I might be able to recover something useful if I had all my tools with me, but I don't. "We're just going to have to let her tell us whenever she's ready."

Kerrington makes it obvious he doesn't like that answer, but what other choice do we have? He tried to fuck it out of her, and that didn't work. We tried being polite and just asking. That didn't work. Patience is all we have left.

"Do you think it's a new fiancé?" he asks.

My gut twists. I hadn't thought of that. "I fucking hope not. Committing murder was not on my bingo card for this month."

Kerrington huffs a laugh and drops onto the couch next to me. I rest my head on his shoulder. "You did great tonight with her. I loved seeing the two of you be like that together."

He tenses next to me. "You weren't scared or repulsed?"

"Not even possible."

"I hurt her," he whispers.

"You fucked her." Squeezing his thigh, I hope it's reassuring. "And it was beautiful."

"She really did sound like she enjoyed it."

"She squirted like a goddamn geyser twice.

Women are so amazing."

He chuckles and kisses the top of my head. "Nicole is a goddess."

"And she's all ours, man. How'd we get so lucky?"

Silence blankets us again and Kerrington's breathing slows down as he drifts off to sleep. I close my eyes and fall under too.

•••

The scent of bacon, coffee, and cinnamon rolls wakes me up. For a hot second, I'm not even sure where I am.

Living room. Hotel suite.

I've somehow been tucked onto the sofa with a blanket and pillow. "Kerrington?"

"He's in the bed, passed out," Nicole says.

There are more clinking and clanking noises.

What the hell is going on? Sitting up, I rub the sleep from my eyes and blink blearily at Nicole. She's got an entire table filled with room service and is currently pouring two cups of coffee. "Eat with me."

Oh, hell yeah.

I shuffle over, smoothing my tangled hair back, and drop into the chair opposite her.

"I wasn't sure what you guys liked, so I ordered one of everything off the menu."

"Perfect." My smile broadens when I see

smoked salmon. "Damn, this is a feast for the gods, sweetheart."

Nicole giggles as she pours hot sauce all over her eggs. "The lox are all yours, Lan. I do not do fish, and I know Kerr's not a fan."

"How do you know that?"

"Because at the gala, you devoured an entire platter of salmon puffs and Kerrington wouldn't go near it."

I build the perfect bite of lox, capers, cream cheese and red onion onto a baguette slice and squeeze a bit of lemon onto it. "Never realized you stalked us so hard, Duchess. I'm flattered."

Shoving the entire thing into my mouth, I almost choke on it when she says, "I've never been able to keep my eyes off either of you."

My throat tightens, fighting my big swallow. I chug some OJ to get it all down. "Oh yeah?"

"I know I always acted like I hated you, but..." Her gaze lifts to mine, holding me hostage. "It's very much the opposite."

My heart clatters in my ribs. Before I go off the rails, drop to my knees, and propose, I clear my throat and ask, "How are you feeling this morning?"

"Really, really, *really* good."

"Not too sore?"

"Nope." She stabs her pancakes and stuffs a huge bite in her mouth. "I slept like a baby, too."

"Did anyone ever tell you it's not ladylike to

talk with your mouth full?"

"Are you accusing me of being a lady?"

We both crack up laughing and I swear I'm eating breakfast with a new version of Nicole I don't think I've ever met before. She's relaxed, content, peaceful, and happy. She's fucking *glowing*.

Kerrington got her this way. I wish he could see her right now, but I'm not about to wake him up. He's a fucking grouch in the mornings.

"Smiles look good on you, girl. You should wear them more often."

Instead of dropping into brat mode and losing that gorgeous grin, she beams even brighter. "I feel so different today. So good."

Morning person or not, I really should wake Kerr up. He's missing this. "Kerrington's going to be relieved."

Her brows knit as she brings her coffee up for a sip. "Why?"

"He let loose on you last night and is still scared he hurt you. He didn't sleep much because he kept his attention on you all night while you slept."

She slowly lowers her cup. "Even after I said I was okay?"

I shrug. "Usually I wouldn't speak for him, or about him like this, but it's important to understand what's going on with us. In this dynamic, we have to look out for each other and take care of each other."

She scoops a dripping, hot sauce drenched spoonful of eggs into her mouth and chews. I'm pretty sure it's just to buy a little time so she can brainstorm a response.

"I have a safe word. And I'm a grown woman."

"Trust me. We're well aware of both those facts."

"He needs to trust me to tell him if it's too much." Her cheeks and neck turn red and I'm already pouring her a glass of water, afraid it's from the hot sauce. "If anything..." she says, stalling out.

Christ, she's turning redder. Should I get the fire extinguisher or something?

"Landon, I um..."

Holy shit, is she going into shock from all the hot sauce? Why does everything have to be so spicy for her, damnit? She's probably losing the lining in her stomach as we speak.

Nicole tucks her hair behind her ears, making them poke out in the cutest way. "Never mind."

"No." I lean forward, concern making heart slam. "What were you going to say?"

"Nothing."

"Nicole." Anger stirs in me because I was so fucking close to having a genuine moment with this woman, and just like always, she's putting walls back up. "Say it. Please."

"Well, it's just that..." She taps her fork on

the edge of her plate. "He thinks he's too rough but…" She clears her throat, and her face reddens like a goddamn tomato. "I would argue he wasn't rough enough. For me. At least."

Pretty sure my soul just left my body.

Her gaze flickers to the bedroom door, and her entire demeanor changes in an instant. "Good morning."

I don't have to turn around to see that Kerrington's awake. Nor do I have to pretend that she didn't just have an open moment with me and now wants to sweep it under the rug because she's embarrassed to admit she's a masochist.

Awww. Bless.

"Good morning, baby." Kerrington strolls over with his sweatpants hung low on his hips and kisses her forehead first, then mine. It's this precise act that makes me fall for him a little more every day.

He's brutal and gentle. Strong and fragile. Just like the rest of us.

Sitting between us, he fills his plate while Nicole pours him a cup of coffee. "What a spread."

"I woke up starving," she says. "Charged the room for all of it, too."

"Good girl." He snags several slices of bacon and then tops off my coffee for me.

Am I living in La-la-land over here? Are we all just going to pretend that there isn't a herd of elephants gathering in the room with us?

There's a mystery caller on a broken phone, along with a masochist, sadist, and switch having breakfast together. I feel like there should be a joke in here somewhere.

"What do you want to do today?" Kerrington swipes his mouth with a napkin and leans back. "Whatever it is, you're getting it."

Great. This is Kerr's way of saying he's sorry for last night.

"Well, I guess we need to start with getting you a new cell phone," I say, butting in before Nicole can respond. "Right?" My eyes dart to her and she mirrors Kerrington's body language. Fantastic. Now I have two hardheads to live with.

"I don't need a new phone yet. It's nice to be unplugged."

"What if there's an emergency?" I press. "Your parents or Grace might need you."

"No one needs me."

Oh, if only she knew how untrue that is.

"We do," Kerrington says. "We fucking need you, Nicole." He reaches under the table, and I think puts his hand on her thigh.

The upbeat, happy girl I dined with a mere five minutes ago vanishes. She shoves away from the table and abandons her breakfast… and us.

My heart stops when I hear the bathroom door shut. Kerrington, however, goes back to eating his meal like nothing's wrong.

"What the fuck?"

"Let her be."

"No." I shove my chair back and stand. "I'm sick of stalling and acting like this doesn't hurt." Storming into the bathroom, I don't even bother knocking. I just plow right in and find her flushing the toilet.

"Landon!"

"Don't do this."

"Don't do what?"

"Shut us out again!" My heart thuds hard in my throat. "I hate that I'm walking on eggshells with you, Nicole. And you know what? I'm glad Kerrington fucked you so hard you couldn't walk last night, because you wear his mark all over your body. He branded you. Maybe I should too, so everyone knows you're ours." Then my petty side shows up. "So *TW* knows you're fucking *ours*."

Her face turns crimson just before all the blood drains from it.

"What the fuck do we have to do to make you understand we love you? That we'll do anything for you? That we *need* you?"

"Lan…"

"Shut the fuck up and let me finish." Christ, I'm such an asshole. But I'm pissed off and can't filter myself. "We've spent nearly a decade watching and wanting you from the sidelines. A decade, woman!" I slam my fist on the counter. "And now you give us a glimpse of what life would be like if we could keep you forever and the instant you start feeling happy about it, you close off."

She shakes her head.

I cup her face, stopping her. "Yes. You do. Out there," I say, pointing toward the dining area. "You were the happiest I have ever seen you, Nicole. And in one minute, when you had to face your truth, you shut us out again."

"I'm not shutting you out," she hisses, smacking my hand away from her cheek. "I'm protecting you, you asshat!"

"Protecting us from what?"

Chapter 25

Nicole

I am in so much trouble.

"Protecting us from *what*?" Landon asks furiously. His blue eyes darken with frustration and concern. I prefer it when they're bright and sparkling. Guess everyone has two sides to their coin. Landon is wildly funny, but also fiercely protective. Kerrington is stoic and intense, but also insecure and cautious.

Me? I'm weak and also stupid.

My brain shoves all the excuses down my throat, and I swallow them. I could say I have this small, insignificant issue handled. I could pull the "it's not your business" card again. I could laugh and play it off like I'm joking. I could lie. I could leave.

I won't do any of those things.

This week with Landon and Kerrington was supposed to be my last hurrah. My final goodbye. My "it was nice knowing you guys, and it's been fun, but I gotta hit the road," and never look back.

As if there was ever a chance I could be so strong?

These two men are my weakness. My kryptonite.

My downfall and my salvation.

I think it took seeing Kerrington break down last night, scared to death that he hurt me, for my eyes to finally open wide. They're not an itch for me to scratch. They're my heartbeat. The air I breathe. The purpose I've been searching for.

"I've been in love with you both for a long time." I'm painfully aware that Kerrington has also now entered the chat. This massive bathroom no longer feels spacious at all. Leaning against the counter, I cross my arms. "I don't know how to say any of this."

"Let's start by getting out of here and into the living room," Kerrington says, all traces of comfort gone from his tone.

My heart clunks as I follow him out, with Landon behind me. Suddenly feeling like a prisoner being escorted to her new cell, I keep my head down and go back into default mode.

Deny, deflect, and disrespect.

Except I can't summon the energy to engage. Keeping this last secret has drained me for too long. If I can share my heart and my body with these two men, why not share my burdens too?

"I'm being blackmailed."

They both become unnaturally still in front of me.

I pretend they're only statues and pour my

heart out.

"After the gala, one particular asshole followed us to the club and took pictures of us. He also got photos of us in the hotel room by the window."

Landon swipes a hand down his face, likely remembering how he fucked my brains out against said window with my tits smashed against the glass.

"He threatened to post the images of us across all social media and send them to the board of directors at my family's firm, as well as every client."

"Jesus fucking Christ." Landon paces like an angry tiger. "Why didn't you say something sooner?"

"I was handling it." The words no sooner leave my mouth when the lie sinks in. I haven't handled it at all. If anything, I've let it eat my self-respect down to the roots. "I didn't tell you because it's personal."

"*How* personal?" Kerrington growls.

Shame wraps its hands around my neck and starts squeezing. "He…" I don't think I can say this out loud without breaking down.

"Did he hurt you? Push himself onto you?"

Landon freezes, waiting for me to answer Kerrington's question. My cheeks get tingly and even my scalp goes numb.

"Why can't we just go back to breakfast? Or last night?" I beg. "Just forget this bullshit and go back to being happy? It's going to be fine. I have it covered."

Kerrington drops to his knees before me and rests his hands on my thighs. "Baby, we need to know what he's done. We can't go back to happy until we know you're safe."

"I *am* safe. I'm here with you, aren't I?"

I'm not about to tell them I pay the fuckhead thousands every month for his silence.

"What about Japan?" Landon asks. "What about when you leave us again?"

My heart hiccups and I feel woozy. "I won't matter after that."

Kerrington's brow digs down. He looks like I just punched him in the gut. "Nicole."

"Don't," I hiss, squeezing my eyes shut. "Please don't press this, Kerrington."

"Give us his name." Landon's voice shakes with anger. "Give. Us. His. Name."

"Why?" I open my eyes and wish I'd kept them closed. Because the looks on their faces kills me. "Please… I'm not worth the trouble I've caused. The press had a field day with me at the gala because they like humiliation. It's just click bait. I'm okay with that and don't care. So, you shouldn't either."

"If you didn't care, you wouldn't be paying them for their silence."

"How did you know I was paying them?" I gawk at Kerrington, feeling too exposed for my own good.

"I didn't until just now, baby."

He fucking tricked me into admitting I'm in deeper than I want to say. And when he pulls me into a hug, I want to bite him.

Instead of taking a chunk of his face off, or pushing him away, I cling to him with all my might. I can't stop shaking. I don't have it in me to shed tears over this, because that pity party ended several months ago. "If he's calling now, he's only upping the amount… or has something new to use against me."

I keep the little detail that the fucker has been stalking me to myself. I'm not trying to get my guys locked up for murder.

Wow. I must be a special kind of delulu if I think either of these men would actually kill for me. Still, I don't want them charged with assault or anything else either. My reputation was trashed long ago. I'm not about to let theirs go in the shitter, too.

"Who else knows about this?" Kerrington asks.

"No one."

"Not even Mason or Grace?"

"Definitely not." I push free from Kerrington's embrace. "And they better *never* find out."

"Your secret is safe with us," he promises, and I want to believe him. But there's an edge to his tone I don't trust.

"*You're* safe with us." Landon sits down

next to me and holds me against him, kissing the side of my head. "Thank you for trusting us enough to tell us this, sweetheart."

All I keep thinking about is how I was so happy this morning. I was so free and joyful and hungry and it's like I was a new, better person.

But chucking my phone off the twenty-seventh floor isn't going to solve my problems. Just like fucking the two loves of my life for a week won't ease the ache in my soul after I leave.

I'm just putting band aids on bullet holes here.

"He won't follow me to Japan," I say, like I have a clue how far this guy will go. "And he didn't touch me, so if you're worried about that, don't be."

"Why does that sound like a half truth?" Landon asks.

Because it is, damnit. "He came to my office late one night. Locked me in a boardroom and tried to coerce me into fucking him. Said if I did, he wouldn't put out the photos."

The tension in the room is so thick, I could cut it with a chainsaw.

"What happened then?" Kerr's voice is so calm, it makes me wince.

"He tried to take what he wanted from me, anyway."

I don't like talking about this.

Landon's hands ball into fists. I keep my attention on Kerrington, if only to let him see how brave I am. "I threw a chair at him and screamed until security came in. He got away, and was wearing a mask, so the surveillance cameras didn't catch him. But he followed me to a coffee shop a couple days later, demanding I give him money, or he'd send out my pics. When I dumped my coffee on him, he posted two articles, which set my career on fire."

"*Greystone Princess rebels with ex-fiancé's best friends,*" Landon recites.

"*Rebound and Reboot - Taking revenge where she can find it.*" Kerrington adds.

I cringe inwardly as shame heats my face. "You saw those?"

"Sweetheart," Landon grabs my hand. "I was the one who took them down."

"Wait. No. My parents paid off some hacker to take all the damning articles down."

"They didn't pay us a dime, baby," Kerrington says quietly. "We did it before they even asked."

I think I'm losing my mind. "No. That… that doesn't make any sense. My mother said she paid some guy an exorbitant amount of money to have it all erased."

"She lied."

The air whooshes out of me. "Why would she lie to me about that?"

"Probably because you wouldn't have believed the truth," Kerrington says, and it's such a blow to my belly. He's right. I would never have expected them to save my ass like that, nor would I have accepted their help.

I had to hit rock bottom to come back to them.

Oh god. They waited for me. I ran away, cut them out, and they still waited for me. They took care of me even when I couldn't see it, didn't know, and didn't ask.

Hot tears burn my eyes. "I don't deserve you."

"Shh." Kerrington pulls me into his chest again and wraps his strong arms around me.

A million questions soar through my foggy brain. I've dragged them into my shitshow, regardless of how much energy, time, and money I've spent trying to keep them out of it.

"Stop paying him," Kerrington orders.

"No! We'll be dragged online. Shunned from our society."

"So what?" Landon huffs next to me. "We don't give a flying fuck about anyone who's not in our immediate family."

"Mason," Kerrington counts on his fingers. "Leah, you. Our family is chosen, and small, and perfect as is. We've never given a shit about what others think of us. You know that, Nicole."

My heart swells. "I didn't think you thought of me in your circle like that."

Kerr's hands fall to my side. "Of course we do. We invite you to everything."

"I figured it was out of pity."

"Does this look like pity to you?" Landon growls. "Does anything we've done with you look pitiful, Nicole?"

Biting my lip, I shake my head. Oh my god, I love them so much.

"What's it look like then?" Landon's tone stays stern. "Come on. Tell us."

"Love."

"That's right, sweetheart." He kisses my forehead.

Kerrington brings us back to the real problem. "You can't pay this guy off forever, Nicole."

"Of course I can."

"And when he ups the amount?" he asks. "What then?"

He's already done that, not that I'll admit it. "I'll figure it out."

"*We.*" Landon stresses. "*We* will figure it out."

They smother me with their big bodies, and good scents, and masculine energy. "I didn't want you to be sucked into my drama."

"Baby, we'll get sucked into anything you're a part of. Happily."

"It's what you do when you love someone, Nicole. You take the good and the bad."

"The ugly and the beautiful," Kerrington says.

"Did... did you just call me ugly?" I fake being mad and smack his arm. "Rude."

Kerrington chuckles, allowing me the small distraction with my terrible attempt at humor. It's enough to let me catch my breath.

"I'm so sorry for everything," I whisper.

He wipes the tear from my cheek with his thumb. "You don't ever have to apologize to us, Duchess. So long as you're being authentic and true, never say sorry for that to anyone."

I've wrestled with my upbringing for as long as I can remember. Yes, it's nice to be stupid rich, but it's not without a major cost. Sometimes I don't think the money is worth it. Not when my personal life is being scrutinized. Not when I'm constantly being judged for what I say, do, wear, eat, where I shop and work, or who I love.

"I love you both so much." Swiping the tears from my face, my fortress builds back up.

"And we love you." Kerrington kisses my head and holds me tighter. "Which means we'll do anything for you, baby. Anything."

"Let us help you," Landon urges again. "*Please.*"

It's the crack in Landon's voice, and the protectiveness trembling in Kerrington's arms, that breaks my walls down and I finally give in.

Chapter 26

Kerrington

She gave us a name. Neither one of us pounced into action immediately, like I'm sure she assumed we would. Nah. That motherfucker can wait a little longer. We're going to give our girl all the comfort and attention she craves for however long she wants it today.

Landon's currently loving life, with our Duchess in his lap, and they're online shopping.

I'm in the shower, hoping the icy water will cool my burning anger.

Newsflash: It doesn't.

Funny, it's usually Landon who loses his temper and I'm normally the calm one in bad situations. But knowing there's some lowlife, piece of shit, cocksucker out there threatening our girl, in any capacity, has me seeing red.

So yeah, I looked up the name she gave me and already have his address, social security number, workplace, as well as license plate and fucking credit card numbers.

I'd love to take the highroad and destroy his

life from the inside out, but that's not punishment enough. He needs a lesson in manners. In person.

Drying off, I can't keep my thoughts straight. How do other people distract themselves from their problems? When I have an issue, it's all I obsess over until it's solved.

So, I dry off and get dressed and join my little family with a fake ass smile on my face and pretend I'm not plotting murder.

Landon looks over at me first, reading my body language like a book, and tenses. "You good?"

"Never better."

He knows I'm lying, and I don't give a fuck. I want Nicole out of New York for good. I want her with us forever. And if she's going to keep her role in the Greystone business and go work overseas, then I guess we're all packing up and moving.

"Do you really want to move to Japan?"

Nicole's brow lifts to her hairline. "Why?"

"Because if so, I need to work on getting us visas."

The relief on Landon's face tells me he's been thinking the same thing. "I meant what I said, Nicole. You're not leaving us again."

Do I sound like a possessive prick? Probably. Do I give a fuck? No.

"You'd move to Japan with me?"

"We'd move to Mars with you," Landon answers for us both. He's not wrong.

"Is that a problem?"

Her shiftiness makes my hands ball into fists. If she denies us this, I don't know how I'll handle it.

Landon senses it too, and his tone changes slightly. "Nicole?"

She visibly gulps like her throat's too tight or something. "I think maybe we should hold off on that for now."

The woman might as well have cut my chest open with a spoon, scooped my heart out, and tossed it over the balcony like she did her fucking cell phone.

"I'm not stalling for reasons you're both probably thinking, so relax."

Relax? Fuck that. "This isn't a light subject like what movie we're going to see tonight. This is our future and your safety we're talking about."

She bites her bottom lip and slides off Landon's lap. "I'm just saying Japan is far."

"The two feet you just moved away from me is too far." Landon's annoyance is obvious.

I agree with him.

Christ, since when did we become complete cave men? This level of possessiveness and protectiveness is over the top, even for us. Then again, is there such a thing as over the top when it involves someone you love?

"What do you want, Nicole?" Leave it to Landon to not beat around the bush. "Just fucking say it so we can all get on the same page."

Wow. That was… brutally to the point. I love him for that.

"It's not that simple."

"Yes, it is," we say at the same time.

She gawks at us for a full count of five, then closes her gaping mouth. "What if what I want isn't what you want?"

"Try us," I say. Because I bet she'd faint if she knew what I truly want for the three of us. Landon might be on the floor with her for all I know.

"I'll sound like a gold digger," she fusses, crossing her arms.

"Honey, there's no such thing as a gold digger. A woman is either in someone's price range or she isn't. And Kerr and I have big bank accounts."

She huffs a little laugh and rolls her eyes. Of course, our money wouldn't impress her. She's probably got double what we have. Only she's not allowed to touch it unless she falls in line with her family's expectations.

Is that her hang up? "Do you not want to be with us because you're afraid you'll be cut off from your accounts?"

Nicole flinches. "I hate that you'd even ask me that." She stands up and storms away from us, but I catch her arm, stopping her. "Then what is it?"

"You're going to think less of me if I say."

"Woman…" I force myself to take in a few steady, calming breaths and remind myself that she may know a lot about us, but there's still a lot left to learn, too. "Do not presume to know everything about me or Landon."

She deflates a little, understanding how insulting that was of her. "Sorry. You're right. It's just my own insecurities running amuck." Letting out a long exhale, she rolls her shoulders back and deadpans me. "I don't want to work for my family anymore. I don't want to work at all. I want to live in a little house with a little pool and mow my lawn and shop for my own groceries."

My heart clogs my throat.

Landon leans forward, and I'd bet a million bucks his mouth is hanging open.

"I want babies. And join that thing that parents go to at the school to bring cupcakes and fundraisers and stuff."

"PTA," Landon says in a gruff voice.

"Yeah. That. And I want to just… be."

"What does *just be* mean exactly?" My body coils so tight, it hurts to breathe. Everything this woman wants is exactly what I've fantasied about for nearly half my motherfucking life.

"I want to just be me. I don't even know what that means yet, but I haven't been me anywhere else except when I'm with you two." Her hands fall to her sides and shoulders droop. "I want to wait at home for you and have dinner waiting at the table. I want to scrub my own stupid toilets. I want to chase our babies around the house with nerf guns and read them bedtime stories."

Landon clears his throat. "And… how does any of this make you a gold digger, exactly?"

"Because I'll have earned none of it!" she says exasperatingly. "I'll just be a kept woman."

"A kept woman," Landon repeats, his gaze slowly swinging to mine. "Do you hear this, Kerr?"

"Ugh!" Nicole stomps her foot. "I'm serious!"

My mind is fucking blown. "Why would we look down on you for this?"

"Because!" She tosses her hands up like we're idiots who can't understand.

Maybe we are.

"So, you're saying you want us to take care of you?" I prowl closer to her.

"I'm saying I want—"

I smash my mouth to hers. Our girl's fingers trace up my back and bury into my wet hair. Tongues dueling, I conquer her easily and love how she submits to me.

Spinning her around, I make her face Landon while I kiss her shoulder and neck, cupping her breasts roughly. She moans against me, leaning back and arching into my touch.

"You don't earn the right to be taken care of by us." Landon closes in like a tiger. "We earn the right to take care of you, Duchess."

She groans when he puts his hands and mouth on her, too. We smother her together. Sandwich her. Worship and adore her.

He unties her robe while I pull it off her shoulders and let it fall to our feet.

"And we'd be the luckiest motherfuckers in the world if we got to come home to you every night." Landon runs his hands through her hair, bringing her in for a kiss.

"And wake up to you every morning." Tracing my hand down her back, I get on my knees.

"God. the thought of you carrying our babies…" Landon sinks to his knees too.

"Filling you with our cum and keeping you in bed for days at a time." I bite her ass cheek playfully. "Watching you grow round with each pregnancy."

"Fuuuuuck." Landon places his hands over mine and we touch her together. Nicole's so keyed up, she's practically vibrating.

I think we just discovered a possible breeding kink between us.

"I won't have any money," she says in a rush. "I'll be cut off if we do this."

"What part of we have big bank accounts are you not listening to, Duchess?"

"But that's *your* money. Not mine," she claps back at Landon.

"Have we not made it crystal clear that we are into sharing?" I sink my hand between her thighs, finding her wet. "Money, pussy, cock, time, baths. We share it all."

"You can spend every dime we make, sweetheart." Landon looks up at her with this big fucking smile on his face. "And have anything else you want from us."

"But..."

"Shut up," he growls, just before burying his face in her pussy.

Nicole stumbles back, leaning into me for balance. I lift her slightly, giving my man better access to her. "And since we're in a wish granting mood, tell us what else you want, baby."

Chapter 27

Landon

My emotions are getting whip lashed today. Good thing I've got stellar coping skills. With my face buried in sweet pussy, my body rocks with a lot of wonderfully chaotic urges. I want to fuck Nicole's brains out, ravish Kerrington, and build a new life for the three of us somewhere we can't be bothered, just so we have extra alone time twenty-four seven. I really need to get on with my search for an island, damnit. But there's another part of me still hung up on the details I memorized earlier about the piece of shit motherfucker threatening our girl. That will be handled accordingly.

I can't believe she's been harboring that secret, dealing with this shit all on her own, for so many months. It makes me rage. It also makes me horny as fuck because damn, she threw a chair at him? And her hot coffee? Our girl is so brave and badass, it makes my dick extra hard.

And how about what she said she wants most is a simple life with babies and all? Fucking perfection.

We've struck gold.

Thank fuck Nicole's got her IUD still in her for now. I want to have fun with our girl before we go filling her with our kids. Oh my god. The vision of little ones running around with Kerrington's dark hair, or my eyes, with Nicole's gorgeous smile makes me want to rip the damn thing out of her right now and get started.

See? Whiplash.

Slow down, Landon. Be a good boy and stay patient. We're young and have plenty of time for everything we want to do.

I lick her cunt like a man on death row who's being served his last meal. Kerrington hooks his arms under her knees and spreads her more for me.

"And since we're in a wish granting mood," he says, "tell us what else you want, baby."

Fuck yeah. Just call me a genie, because these two are definitely rubbing me the right way. Her pussy is so sweet and swollen already and the growls coming out of Kerrington are music to my ears.

Nicole gasps when I sink a couple fingers inside her, pumping and twisting them slowly. "I want… fuuuuuck I can't think straight when you do that, Lan."

"Stop." Kerrington's tone is all I need to hear, and I back off. Waiting on my knees, I look up at her patiently. "Can you think straight now?"

Her breasts heave with every breath she takes, and her eyelids are hooded with lust. She licks her lips, looking like she's about to say something.

"Say it, baby, and it's all yours." Kerrington gently sets her down but won't stop touching her. I flashback to the night on the dance floor at the club when my hands had a mind of their own and I couldn't keep them off our beautiful girl. This woman is addictive in all the ways—her taste, her laugh, her smell, her touch, the way she blushes and all the pretty little noises she makes.

Hungry for another taste, I stand up to kiss her, sucking that fat bottom lip of hers between my teeth. Then I pinch her nipples and press my forehead to hers, feeling mighty motherfucking greedy.

"Let us give you what you need, Duchess." I collar her throat and kiss her again, taking control.

"I... fuck, Trick." She gasps when I twist her nipples again while Kerrington fingers her from behind. "Oh my god, I can't... shit... wait."

We both pause.

"Anything at all?" she tests us.

I answer with another pinch and pull on her hard nipples. She cries out in half pleasure, half pain, and I know that I'm not nearly as rough as Kerrington was with her last night. But seeing her responsiveness leads me to believe I'm also able to give her what she craves in the same way he can, just at a different level.

"I want Kerr to fuck you… while you… fuck me."

Be still my two-person-loving heart.

Look, I have no idea what I did in a past life to deserve what I'm getting in this one, but it's obvious I was a fucking hero.

"Done," Kerrington says, knowing damn well I'm on board with that.

I pick up our woman and carry her into the bedroom, relishing how she wraps her legs around my waist and kisses me like her life depends on our connection.

Kerrington lubes up while I go down on Nicole for a little while longer. I can't help it. She tastes and smells so good. Honestly, do women understand the spell they put us under with what's between their thighs?

"I want you in my mouth." She digs her hands through my hair.

"As you wish." I climb up her body to feed her my straining cock. The instant her hot mouth wraps around me, I'm seeing stars. Holy mother of —

"Get back here," Kerrington says, literally dragging me off our Duchess. His playfulness makes a laugh bubble out of me. I've never felt so light and free, which is saying something. Just when I think I can't love these two any harder, I fall down a deeper level.

"I want him inside me first," she says to

Kerrington. "And I want to watch his expression when he takes you inside him."

I think I'm going to stroke out. My heart pounds so hard, my ears have a pulse. To hear her give demands makes me so fucking proud of her.

Kerrington grabs my throat, tipping my head back to kiss me, then he growls against my mouth. "Let her pussy stretch around that big dick. Make her come for both of us while I fuck you."

Nodding is the only thing I can do, because my brain cells have exploded. This isn't the first time we've done this together, but it's more amplified now. We're all on the same page, finally, and the energy is entirely different. It's no longer just our bodies connected, it's everything else, too.

She's so wet and ready. I use her arousal as lube and slowly push my way inside her. Nicole's eyes widen with each thrust I make, feeding her an inch at a time until I slam home. Her sharp gasp lets me know it hurts a little. I've hit her cervix. "You okay?"

"Never better." Wrapping her arms around my neck, she brings me in for a scorching kiss and I rock into her slowly. Deliberately. Holding my hand out, I don't have to wait long before the vibrating wand hits my palm. *Thank you, Kerrington.*

Teamwork makes the dream work, right?

Turning it on to the lowest setting, I hold it

against her clit and fuck her deep and steady. She claws the mattress, her eyes locked on mine until she's about to explode, and then she looks at Kerrington. Her pussy gets a vise grip on my dick when she comes for us.

"You're so beautiful." I lean down for a kiss, bracing for what happens next.

Bracketing her face with my hands, I stare down at her while Kerrington pushes himself into my ass. I've got the best of both worlds right now.

"So are you," Nicole says, cupping my face while I take Kerrington.

I'm a live wire. Electricity flows through me, lighting up my vision and jump starting my body.

Kerrington runs his rough fingers down my back and holds my hips, but I'm the one setting the pace. Rocking back and forth, I fuck her and fuck myself with Kerrington.

It's perfection.

Riding that high for as long as I want, I kiss them both and enjoy their hands on me. Their tongues. Their breath. Their mouths.

Nicole coils up again and I pound into her a little harder, helping her reach another release. But god damn, I want Kerrington to go a little harder on me too. "Give me more," I say over my shoulder.

Kerr doesn't need to be told twice. He pops off his knees and balances on his feet, hovering above us, then slams into me. "Like this?"

I let myself get shoved into Nicole from

Kerrington's force. "Fuck yeah." I look down at Nicole. "Are you okay with this?"

"Definitely." Her eyes are big and bright and look like they did this morning when she was happy at breakfast. The smile on her face only fades when she screams from another orgasm.

"God damn, she's so fucking tight when she squeezes."

"You like feeling me come around you?" Our Duchess asks, fishing for compliments I'll gladly feed her all day, every day, for the rest of my life.

"Yeah, I do. I've never felt anything better."

"Is that so?" Kerrington growls from behind me. "Guess I better step up my game, then."

I knew that would spur him into competition mode.

I'm winning at life today, guys.

Between the wet noises of her pussy, and the slapping of my ass against Kerrington, I'm a goner.

Kerr grabs a handful of my hair and pulls. "I didn't say you could come yet."

"Fuuuuuck." How does he always know when I'm close? "Please?"

He kicks up his pace, forcing the air out of my lungs. It's overwhelming, which I love. "Beg harder, baby."

I didn't earn my brat title for nothing. Clenching my jaw, I keep quiet and fuck them both until my vision tunnels and my release reaches a breaking point. "Please," I beg, like the good boy I am. "Please let me come now."

Nicole's cunt clamps around me and she makes this delicious noise that says hearing us turns her on.

So, I beg even more.

"I can't hold it much longer, Daddy. Let me come inside our Duchess." Kerrington fucks me so deep, I roar with pleasure. "Fuck. Please. I can't hold it."

"We're coming together," he grunts. "Just… let me…" *Slam, slam, slam.* The bed rocks with our force and Nicole's fingers dig into my thighs as she holds onto me, taking it.

I won't last much longer. It feels too good. Too intense. Too perfect.

"Come for us," Kerrington commands, hitting my pleasure point and riding me hard as I drive into Nicole. He smacks my ass, setting me aflame, and I roar with my release.

The only thing louder is the way Kerrington loses his control too.

My dick throbs, pumping Nicole with all my cum while Kerrington does the same to me. When it's over, I collapse slightly, careful not to crush our girl under us. Kerrington pulls out, and the instant he's gone, I feel empty and wrung out. It's all good. I'm buzzing in a really great headspace because of it.

"You okay?" I ask Nicole, checking in.

"Oh yeah," she practically purrs.

I pull out slowly and kiss her. "You did so good for us, Duchess."

The praise lights her face up in the best way. "You did really good for us too, Trick."

"Here." Kerrington hands me a wet cloth. But before I can clean up our girl, he playfully pushes me away and says, "I'm on clean up this time, fucker." He leans down and licks her pussy, lapping up what leaks out.

"What's this for then?" I twirl the towel.

"Yourself."

"Oh hell no." I grab a handful of his hair and pull him back. "You can clean me up too."

Kerrington arches his brow at me. Then, with a wicked smile, he sucks my half-hard cock all the way down his throat. The tip of his tongue swipes against my balls, and I suck in a harsh breath. That sensation, paired with his cum leaking out of my backside, is fucking heady shit.

I feel dizzy.

Nicole rolls over onto her side, propping her head on her elbow to watch us. The hunger in her eyes makes me want to fuck Kerrington's face.

Which is exactly what I do.

He takes most of it too, until I fully harden, and the back of his throat turns into a wall I hit over and over. He gags on me, which I'm a big fan of. Grabbing the base of my cock, he strokes me fast and sucks me off until I blow again. The orgasm shudders through me, making the hair on my arms stand up. My nipples harden and spine bows. "Fuuuuuck."

He drains me dry, and I collapse back on the bed.

Nicole giggles, curling against me like she's the big spoon. "You're so pretty when you orgasm, Landon."

I have no clue what to say to that.

"He makes the best faces when he detonates, doesn't he?" Kerrington asks, snuggling up on my other side.

"Totally."

I flip them both the bird and settle in for a nap, because I'm too tired to clean myself up or do much else at the moment. Sandwiched between the loves of my life, I doze off, hoping this is what my future will be like, knowing when I wake up, I'll take care of the only thing standing in our motherfucking way.

Chapter 28

Kerrington

I'm in no mood to sleep, but I'm happy to see Nicole's passed out. I think after she unburdened herself and told us everything, she's finally able to catch up on her sleep, especially knowing we'll keep her safe. Of course, all those orgasms we gave her probably helped, too. I'm also relieved to see her appetite coming back. That spread for breakfast really eased some of my worry. Especially with how she shoveled each bite in.

Our girl is on the mend, she's safe, and she's staying with us. I'll give her every damn thing she wants from this day forward. Nicole wants a life that's so spectacularly normal, it melts my heart. I honestly never planned on having kids or a cookie cutter life. But that's only because it just didn't seem in the cards for me and Landon. I always imagined we'd be cruising through our life together, traveling, negotiating new business deals, and curled in each other's arms at night in a top tier penthouse with sleek leather furniture and glass tables.

I was happy enough with that future because I never dared to dream something beyond it. And now we have Nicole.

We're going to eventually have crayons rolling across the floor, and piles of dirty laundry, weeds in the garden, and tons of shoes scattered by the front door. The TV will play in the background constantly with some kind of annoying cartoon and crumbs will be smashed into the carpet.

Fucking Hell, I can't wait.

Too restless to sleep, I carefully get out of bed and make my way to the cold breakfast left on the table. Picking at a croissant, I pour a cup of coffee and grab my laptop. Everything Landon could find in his five-minute search is in a document still open on my screen.

The man giving Nicole shit is in his mid-thirties, single, and—

Something strange makes a sound in the living room. Our suite is big, but it's also dead quiet, so the slightest noise can be heard. In my peripheral, I notice movement by the door.

What the fuck is that?

As quietly as I can, I snatch the envelope that's been stuffed under our door. It's from the hotel, so it's most likely a bill. Opening the damned thing, my heart stops.

It's not a bill. It's…

"Fuck." Rage courses through my veins as I

glare at the photos taken of Nicole, me, and Landon the other night on the balcony. She's naked and handcuffed to the railing. My head's thrown back while I fuck her. Landon's to the side, holding a toy with one hand, his dick in the other.

Picture after picture has my vision tunneling.

There's a sticky note on the last one that says, "Cinnamon Café Noon" and I'm already swinging open the door to catch this mother fucker with my bare hands. But no one is there.

Of course not.

Heading into the bedroom to get Landon, I find him already awake.

Sitting up and stretching his arms, he smiles at me. But when he sees the look on my face, his body kicks into serious mode. "What's wrong?"

I press my finger to my lips, make a *Shh* gesture, and have him follow me out to the living room. Stuffing the envelope in his hand, I quickly grab our clothes while he reviews what's inside it.

Tossing him a shirt and pants, I swiftly get dressed myself. Nicole's still passed out, and I hope she stays that way until we get back. I'd rather take care of this before she awakens because I know she'll try to stop us from what we're about to do. Or join.

Landon's fuming. "Where the fuck did this come from?"

"It was slid under the door just now." In a rush to leave, I grab Nicole's car key and beeline for the exit with Landon hot on my heels.

He's still trying to get his boots on when we hit the elevator. My heart races and I push the lobby button a million times before the damned thing starts moving.

"There's no way he made it up here and delivered that shit himself."

Landon's right. The hotel is discreet and too private to let anyone up to our suite. You need a special card key just to get past the fifth floor.

The elevator takes a lifetime to bring us to the ground level, and when the doors open, we head straight for the front desk.

"I'll do the talking," Landon says quietly. "You look like you're about to rip someone's face off."

Because I am.

And I know Landon well enough to understand that the tension in the tendons of his neck and the fake fucking smile on his face means he's going to try to beat me to the first punch.

"Good afternoon," Landon says with all the charm his murderous ass can muster. "Can you tell me who might have delivered something to our room just now?"

The woman looks terrified and face drains of color.

Great. Landon's scaring her. And I'll likely do worse because I have no charm when it comes to this shit.

"Umm, that was me," she answers in a tiny voice. "I'm so sorry if I disturbed you." Tears fill her eyes, and she panics. "Please don't get me fired. It's my first week here and I—"

"Hey, whoa, no, no, no." Landon pulls out his best smile and calms her down. "I just was curious about the person who gave it to you."

"He-he-he was young. Maybe thirteen, I guess? He said you were his dad and that he was sending tickets up to you for a show later this evening. I… I didn't think to ask questions. Our guest's privacy is important."

"It's fine. Totally fine. Thank you so much." Landon waves off whatever else she was going to prattle, and we beeline for the front door.

"He hired a kid to do his dirty work," I seethe. The car is just ahead of us, so I clutch my key and pull out my… "Fucking Hell. I left my cell in the room."

"Already got it pulled up." Landon waves his cell at me, with the map to the Cinnamon Café ready.

It says it's fifteen minutes away.

We make it there in six.

Marching into the coffee shop, I see my target sitting in the corner, facing us. It's not hard to pick out the problem. He's staring at us with a smug fucking smile I'm about to punch off his goddamn face.

Without introductions, I storm over and

haul the motherfucker up, hoping I pop his shoulder out of the socket, and frog-march his ass right outside.

"We're Bounty Hunters," Landon explains to the baristas, who I assume are gawking at us. "Have a nice day!"

I drag this piece of shit into the alley and slam him against the brick wall.

Then I punch him in the nose.

"Kerrington, where are your manners, bro?" Landon knocks me out of the way and slugs the fucker in the gut, making him double over, then upper cuts him in the jaw. "You gotta do a combo deal or the message doesn't really click. Try again."

He side-steps out of my way and the guy charges me, driving me backwards until I hit a dumpster.

"Boys, boys, we can't make a lot of noise, mkay? That's how cops are called. And we don't want the cops called, do we, *Tim*?" Landon wraps his arm around Tim's throat and jerks him off me. "Let's play nice for a minute before we go back to having fun."

"Fuck you," Tim snarls. Blood pours from his broken nose and his beanie halfway hangs off his head, about to fall off.

Landon tugs it down, fixing it for him, and slaps him on the back. "How's it going, Timothy Barron Wade of 16 Crispin Lane? Is your sister Jenny doing okay? I'm sure teaching third grade must be brutal."

His face pales.

"Aww, look at him, Kerr. He thought he was the only one who knew how to use the internet and a camera." Landon pulls his cell out and starts flipping through photos he snagged from Tim's social media accounts. They were set to private, but Landon has ways around that.

"So, what is it you wanted to see us about?" Landon fishes. "You need another photo op or something?"

"I'll blast it." Tim wipes his nose, smiling with a bloody mouth. "I'll blast those pictures everywhere and ruin you."

"Is this guy precious or what?" Landon puts his arm around him like they're old pals.

"Why would we care?" I ask cautiously.

Tim scoffs. "The Greystone Heiress getting railed by her ex-fiancé's two business partners would make headlines in all the celebrity news. I'd be famous for that credit."

"So, post it," Landon shrugs.

"What?"

"You heard me. Post it."

"Why? So, you can take it down like I'm sure you did my other articles?" Tim spits on the ground by my feet. "No, that bitch needs to pay. She cost me my job."

I clock him in the jaw, sending him tumbling, but Landon's grip on his arm is strong enough to keep him upright.

"Call her that again and I'll split your skull."

"I'd watch your manners," Landon cautions him. "Kerrington's a grouch when he doesn't get enough sleep."

"What do you want?" I ask.

"A million for my silence."

That makes me laugh. "Cutting out your tongue would be faster and also guarantees your silence." I crowd him while Landon holds him so he can't run. "And I'll take every finger you have too." Just to drive home my point, I snatch his hand, yank it behind his back, and break two of his fingers in a blink.

Tim howls in pain, but Landon covers his mouth. "Shh, don't be a little bitch."

"You will not go near Nicole, me, or Landon ever again. You will not have any contact with our friends or family or anyone we do business with." I get in his face, pressing my forehead to his, crowding him even more. "If I even so much as catch a *whiff* of your nauseating cologne anywhere near our girl, her home, the stores she shops in, the restaurants she eats in, or even the street she walks down, I will fucking kill you. Do you understand?" Tim's eyes blow wide with panic when I press a blade to his throat. "Are. We. Clear?"

"Crystal," he sputters, trembling.

"Get out your phone."

Tim trembles while searching his pockets for his cell.

"Wire Nicole the money you took from her," I growl. "Now."

"I can't. I don't have it."

Pressing the blade harder to his throat, I'm perilously close to slicing. "You really want to lie to us right now, cocksucker?"

"Account one-four-double-oh..." Landon recites the fucker's bank account number and balance down to the penny, making Tim's expression go from terrified to sick.

"We only had five minutes to spare earlier, or I'd have your entire life memorized and at my disposal to destroy." I twist the knife against him. "Now give her back her motherfucking money."

Landon holds the phone out to Tim's face and unlocks the screen himself. Then he taps a few things and stuffs his phone back into Tim's pocket. "There, I did it for you. See, was that so hard?"

"Fuck you," Tim snarls.

Landon elbows him in the face before tossing his hands up at me, looking exasperated. "This guy seriously has no manners."

"I know who you are," Tim says to him, stumbling back to his feet. "You're the youngest of five. Have four older sisters and grew up in a tiny trailer in Maine." He turns to me next. "And you? With your family's bourbon distillery and horse farm in Kentucky. Your parents sent you off to live with your grandmother in Connecticut when you were ten."

I'm struggling to understand why he thinks any of this is relevant. "Are you trying to be relatable, or do you think it's trivia night, my guy? Because you're not saying anything mind-blowing here."

"He's bragging that he's done his research on us."

"Big whoop."

Tim grins. "I know a lot about the two of you. And Mason, Gage… *Leah.*"

"Oh helllll no." Landon punches him again. "You keep her name out of your mouth, too."

Tim spits a tooth out this time. "I'm going to sue you. Have you arrested for assault and battery."

"Go ahead. Call the cops." I tip my head and smile. "Because we've got enough money to make bail and get damn good lawyers. But you? Not so much. We'll have you charged with aggravated assault, sexual harassment, stalking, blackmail, bribery of a minor, and…"

"Fine." Tim yanks his arm out of Landon's grip. "Fine! I won't go near her again."

"We'll know if you do," I warn. "And god help you if that happens."

Tim tugs on his winter coat and stares at the ground. "I didn't mean for it to go this far. I just…" He blows out a long sigh. "Fucking hell. I have no excuse. I was just greedy and power hungry and stupid."

"Get therapy," Landon says in a dull tone.

"Because if you step out of line again, you won't be meeting us in a café or an alley. You'll be a goddamn coffin."

Tim backs away. "Yeah. Okay. Alright." He bumps into a stack of cardboard boxes and catches himself. "I'm sorry, okay? Tell her I'm sorry and she won't have any problems with me again."

"Yeah, see, that's not good enough." I stalk towards him, peeling my coat off and dropping it on the ground. "You still have to apologize for trying to push yourself on her in her office."

Landon and I work like two wolves circling dinner.

Then we close in.

Chapter 29

Nicole

Kerrington's cell going off wakes me from our little nap. Wait. Where are they?

His cell dings again and then it rings. Snagging it from the bedside table, I stare at a number I never thought I'd seen on Kerrington's phone.

"Mom?"

"Oh, thank heavens!" she exclaims. "Nicole, we've been worried sick!"

Sighing, I cover myself up with a sheet, even though I know she can't see me. "Sorry, I didn't mean to worry you. I just needed a break from everything and came to Mason's for a little while."

"Don't lie to me, Niki. You're not there for Mason."

The silence between us makes me feel like a child in trouble and I have to give some sorry excuse for my actions. But I won't. I'm going to fess up and tell the truth.

Then I'll take Mason's advice and walk away.

My heart is already breaking because I love my parents, and I don't want this to be the end. But I know when I say what I want, and what I'm going to do, they'll disapprove, make me choose, and my life will become very different moving forward.

"I'm in love with Kerrington…" My mouth runs dry. "And Landon." The pause while I wait for her response is enough to make me break out in a sweat. "Did you hear me, Mom?"

"Of course, I heard you." Her voice is too calm, and that makes me scared. "And how do they feel about you?"

"They love me too. We want a life together."

"The three of you?"

"Yes."

"At the same time?"

"Yes." How else did she see that going? "I'm sorry."

Again, another long pause. Then my mom sighs and I can hear her pouring a drink for herself. "Sweetpea, what on earth are you apologizing for?"

"I'm sure this isn't how you thought my life would go."

"True, but that doesn't mean you owe anyone an apology for it. It's *your* life, Nicole. Your father and I only want what's best for you."

"And you thought making me marry Mason was best? Or *Jackson*?"

"I never agreed to have you marry Mason's

brother. Scarlett went off the rails that night at the gala, and I've never forgiven her for it. You and Jackson would have been a hideous couple."

I think that was her attempt at a joke, but I'm too scared to laugh. "Are you saying you're fine with me being with two men at once?" That came out wrong, didn't it? Shit.

"Are you saying they're going to treat you like a princess and give you the life you deserve?"

I swallow past the lump in my throat. "Yes. God, yes, Mom. That's all they want to do."

"Then that's all we want for you, darling. Your happiness is all we've cared about."

I think I'm still sleeping, and this is all a dream. Has to be. The fact that Landon and Kerrington are nowhere to be seen in the suite is yet another clue that this isn't real. So, I go for gold. "I don't want to work for Greystone anymore, either. I don't want to work at all."

"I think that's best as well," she responds with tension in her tone.

"Why? Because I haven't done a good enough job?"

"No." I hear her take a sip of her drink. Bet its whisky, neat. From Kerrington's family's distillery. He sends her a bottle of it every year for her birthday. "We think you've done a fine job, Nicole. But you've run yourself into the ground, and that is not okay."

My defenses go up. "I'm only doing what Dad asks of me."

"Which has been a bone of contention between us these past six months. He's allowed you to work yourself into a tailspin."

"And yet *you* were the one to suggest I relocate to Japan for our business!"

"Only because I could see you were so unhappy here, Niki. My god, you're like a machine with no soul."

Tears prick my eyes, because that hurts.

"I've watched you waste away ever since the gala. You're pushing yourself too far. Proving yourself to God knows who and for no good reason."

"No good reason?" My temper flares and the first tear falls. "I was humiliated that night! And have been blackmailed ever since." Before she can ask about it, I talk over her. "I gave up my chance at happiness to be wedded to Mason motherfucking Finch, all because you and his family are so greedy and untrusting."

"Nicole," she warns with her mom voice.

"I'm not done." Standing up, I pace. "Why would you force me to move to the other end of the world if you're this upset that I'm working so much to begin with? Is it because you're ashamed of me, too? All those articles got scrubbed from the internet but not from your brain, is that it?"

"Absolutely not." Her tone and pitch match mine with hostility. "I don't give a damn what the articles say. They're click bait and no one cares."

"Your friends care. The country club

members care. Dad's partners care."

"Is that what you think?" she huffs.

"I heard dad call me a whore."

"He'd never call you such a thing."

"He did. I heard him. It broke my fucking heart."

"Then he and I will have words once I hang up."

Silence spreads between us.

"Niki, I don't give a damn about any of that gala nonsense. I only wish you would be the same way."

I'm struck stupid. "Mom." This dream has gone off the rails. Leaving the suddenly too tiny bedroom, I pace in the living room instead. "You said you paid to have the articles wiped."

"I certainly would have, but Kerrington and Landon took care of it before I even had the chance. They refused to accept money for their service, too."

"I know," I say, pinching the bridge of my nose. "But why go through all that effort if you don't care what people think?"

"Because *you* care," she claps back. "We did it for *you*, Nicole."

I have to sit back down. "But..."

"And now you're telling me you've been blackmailed? Ugh, I'll bet my diamond collection it's that reporter from the HBK Daily. What was his name... Tim something."

"Timothy Wade," I say, feeling my cheeks

grow numb.

"Fucking twatstick. I should have had security teach him a lesson a long time ago. I'll be making calls and putting an end to that man by midnight."

But I don't hear what she says after that because my blood is swishing too loudly in my ears. The world stops spinning. I think the sun stops shining too. My vision dims, zeroing in on a stack of photos sitting on the coffee table along with a note that has some café written on it.

"Oh my god." Picking up the pictures, my blood starts to boil.

"Nicole Antoinette Greystone, are you listening to me?"

No, I'm not. "Sorry, Mom. What?"

The door opens and in walks Kerrington and Landon with blood all over their outfits.

I think I'm going to pass out.

"I said I want you happy and safe. If Kerrington and Landon are the ones to make you that way, then you have our blessing."

This isn't a dream. It's a nightmare.

The photos fall out of my hand and onto the floor. I can't feel my legs when I try to stand and walk over to them.

"Scarlett lost Mason and Grace because of the way she treated them. She'll likely lose Jackson, too, if he has any sense," my mom says, having no clue what I'm looking at. "She loves no one but herself, but we love you more than anything in the world, Niki. Dad and I want you happy. And I will not lose you just because I wanted a different path for you that you're not willing to take. I'm not disappointed, baby. I'm proud of you."

I can't think straight.

Kerrington sits down on the couch and pulls me into his lap. Landon's hovering over the discarded breakfast, plucking fruit and popping grapes in his mouth.

I think I've lost my goddamn mind.

"Every parent wants their child happy, Nicole. My only wish for you is that you've finally found it."

"I have," I say numbly.

"Good. Now tell those boys I'll be seeing them at Christmas this year, understand me?"

I nod, dumbfounded. "Yes."

"I love you, Niki."

"Love you, too."

She hangs up and I honestly have no idea where the cell I'm holding goes because it's suddenly out of my hands and Kerrington's kissing me.

"What happened?" I ask once he comes up for air. As far as I can tell, there isn't a scratch on either of them, so why is there blood all over their clothes?

Ignoring my question, Kerrington kisses me again and rolls me onto my back, already unbuckling his pants.

"I need to get inside you, baby."

"Are you hurt?"

"No." His kisses are desperate and make me dizzy.

"Landon?"

"Right here, Duchess." He peels his shirt off and joins us. "You're going to have to give him some alone time first, though. He's been through it this morning."

Kerrington's like a wild animal, kissing, biting, licking me. I've seen him turned on before, but this is next level, even for him. It awakens this primal part of me that I've only ever let these two see. "Harder. Bite me harder."

His teeth sink into my neck and white stars burst in my vision. My pussy floods. "Again."

"Don't want to hurt you."

"You can't," I say, coaxing him to put his mouth on me again. "I want you to bite hard enough, so when I touch it tomorrow, I get flashbacks of today."

"Fuuuck." Kerrington sinks his teeth into me again, and my hips instantly rise to meet his pelvis. "What's your safe word, baby?"

"Teapot." My heart hammers in my chest when he presses his dick against my pussy, seeking entrance.

"Use it if I start to go too far. Promise?" Kerrington waits, hovering over me, until I say okay.

Then he slams into me like a rutting beast.

It's brutal. Wonderful.

And the very real possibility that they met Tim and took care of him, just to protect me, sends me right over the edge.

"I love you," I say while he fucks me harder and harder. "I love you both so much."

Landon wraps his hand around my throat and tips my head back, kissing me. "We love you too, sweetheart."

I've never felt so high.

"We won't let anything happen to you ever again." Landon runs his hands through my hair, kissing me while Kerrington pulls out.

"Turn around and sit on my lap, Duchess."

I'm on cloud nine as I do what I'm told. Facing the same way Kerrington is, I ease down, impaling myself on his dick, and lock gazes with Landon. "You too," I say breathlessly.

"Fucking hell." Landon pumps his length, and I momentarily panic because I have no clue if he'll be able to fit, but I want to try. "Kerr?"

"What she wants, she gets. That's the rule." He reaches over and grabs Landon's cock, forcing him to climb onto the sofa so he can suck it first.

Then I join him. It's a crowded situation but Kerrington and I licking Landon's dick together makes me so wet, I can't stand it. "Inside me. Now."

What's a girl got to do for a little DVP, damnit?

"If it's too much, say the word." Landon

positions himself in front of us and I plant my feet on either side of Kerrington's thighs, spreading myself as wide as I can.

"That's it," he says, coaching me through it. "Just stay relaxed for us. You're taking us so well, Duchess." He works his fingers into me, stroking himself while stimulating me and Kerrington simultaneously. When he gets three fingers in, Kerr makes inhuman noises behind me.

"I think he likes that," I tease.

Landon pulls out and licks his fingers. "Mmm. Then he's in for a treat." He presses the tip of his dick against my pussy and starts working his way in, talking me through it.

"That's it, baby. You're taking us so well." His head pushes in and I feel my pussy stretch. There's a twang of pain, but it shoots pleasure through my body.

"That's our girl. Stay relaxed… just like… just like that. I'm halfway in, sweetheart."

My head's spinning. Sandwiched between them, I feel like the most powerful woman on the planet.

"That's our good girl. That's our good… fucking… girl."

They're both inside me completely now.

I can't breathe, let alone move.

"You were made to take us both," Kerrington growls against my back.

I think he's right.

We work slowly, moving carefully until we

find a rhythm that works.

"I feel so full." Leaning against Kerrington, I let them have their way with me.

"Your dick is so fucking hot against mine," Landon groans. "And our Duchess is so goddamn wet."

He rubs my clit in slow circles with his thumb while Kerrington pinches and twists my nipples.

I detonate.

The orgasm is so strong I think it tears me apart, breaking me into a million screaming pieces that are all floating like atoms in space. It lasts far longer than any orgasm I've ever had, too.

"Fill me up," I beg, like the greedy girl I am. "Please fill my pussy with all your cum."

Landon leans forward, cupping the back of my head, and kisses me. His hips turn to pistons and Kerrington's under me, doing the same. The image of what this must look like drives my arousal to new levels of unhinged.

I know the minute Landon unloads because his entire body shudders and he lets go of my head to grip Kerrington instead. I'm sandwiched between them, in perfect position to bite Lan's nipple. He roars with his release, flooding me, and Kerrington follows suit.

Kerr groans.

Their dicks throb, twitching as they pour into me. I think I'm going to pass out.

Collapsing on Kerrington, he bears all my weight while Landon holds my face. "Are you okay?"

"Never… better…" Adrenaline drains out of me like a sieve, leaving me exhausted. "I feel so floaty and tingly."

He pulls out first, making me wince. "Shit. You still good?"

I giggle. "Yes."

Kerrington gently lifts me off his lap and the absence of them feels like a tremendous loss inside me. Licking my lips, still in my little happy world, I stuff my fingers inside myself to keep their cum there a little longer.

"Fuck me sideways, you're gonna be the death of us." Landon kisses me first, then Kerrington.

"Well, at least we'll die happy," Kerrington laughs.

Chapter 30

Kerrington

Nicole leans into the mirror to apply her makeup. "Are you going to tell me what happened?"

We're going over to Mason and Leah's, finally, to finalize the new payment system program we coded for the Brazen Bunny. Once I show Mason how it works and get their final approval, we're all having dinner together.

"Isn't ignorance bliss?" I don't want to tell her all the details, because I'm worried she'll think less of me because of the way I acted. Except, holding information from her feels wrong.

"I want to know." Closing her eyes, she sets her makeup with some kind of spray and fans her face.

"He asked us for a million dollars, and we declined to pay."

She gulps, busying herself by digging out lipstick from her bag next. "And then what?"

"We taught him a lesson in manners."

"Manners are important."

"Extremely." I can't tell if she's scared or turned on about it. "He won't be coming for you or anyone we are even remotely familiar with ever again."

"Is he dead?"

"No."

"Landon said you used a knife on him."

The snitch! "It was a butter knife from our breakfast. Still had your pancake syrup sticking to it."

Nicole cracks a laugh that makes me less hostile. "You're kidding."

I shrug. "It's all I had. I left so fast I didn't think about anything other than getting my hands on the fucker. But he definitely thought I had a big one."

"You do have a big one." My spicy girl grabs my dick through my pants and squeezes.

"Hey, hey, hey." Landon storms in with a bottle of water. "Don't get him started. We're late already." He sets the water in front of Nicole. "Drink five sips, Duchess."

She picks it up and obeys.

"Why do you listen to him and give me nothing but bratty behavior?"

"I like the rewards I get from you both when I act accordingly." Nicole winks at me through the mirror and leaves the bathroom, giving both of us a spectacular view of her bare ass that still rocks my handprints from an hour ago.

Christ, my dick is so fucking hard.

"Don't even *think* of going for round four," Landon warns. "We can't cancel on Mason again. Leah's been waiting on us, too."

He's right. Damnit. "Five minutes."

"No."

"Three."

"Motherfucker, you've never come that fast in your life. Don't pretend you can now."

He's right.

"Let's go, boys!" Nicole calls out from the main area.

I tip my head back and groan. "Neither of you are playing fair."

"Yes, we are." Landon hits the button on the remote control, making the toy up my ass buzz faster. "Let's go. Chop, chop."

I'm not going to survive this.

The only reason I'm doing it at all is because Nicole put it on her fucking wish list.

That's right. Her wish list. And Landon and I are going to grant her every single thing on it. So here I am, already breaking out in a sweat, heading to my best friend's house for work, when I want to be…

"Shit." My arms fly out and I brace against the doorjamb of the bathroom. "I can't do this."

Landon spins around. "Are you tapping out?"

"No." I just can't fucking move either. "Give me a second."

Nicole saunters over like a bad little vixen. I

hold her gaze while Landon switches the settings on me again.

The noise I make is ungodly.

My girl drops to her knees and unbuckles my belt, freeing my dick in seconds. "Trick, help me?"

"As if you have to ask, Duchess."

While I hold myself up, these two work together to suck me off. I blow my load in less than a minute.

"Well, that's a first," Landon teases, stuffing me back into my pants. "See? Not always easy to keep control, is it?"

I flip him the bird.

Nicole laughs with her whole body, and I help her stand. Jerking her into my chest, I tip her chin and kiss her until we're both mindless animals again. She brings out the best, worst, craziest parts of me and I love her for it.

"Sometimes control should be broken," I say, turning my attention to Landon. He brings out the strongest, weakest, greatest parts of me, and I love him for that too. "Besides, breaking things is my passion."

"Tell me about it," Nicole purrs. "My pussy will never be the same after what you two have done to it."

Landon and I both freeze, and my stomach drops.

"Relax," she says, slapping my arm playfully. "It's a good thing."

I cock my eyebrow. "You sure about that?"

"One hundred percent." Nicole fixes her sapphire earrings and winks at me. "Some toys like to be broken."

"You're right." Landon rubs the back of his neck. "She's gonna be the death of us."

"Sissies." Nicole spins around and saunters towards the door. We follow like two spellbound fools. Proudly.

"If you're a good girl, maybe I'll break you again later tonight," Landon teases, running his hand over her ass.

"And if you're a good boy..." I grab a handful of his hair before kissing him. "Maybe I'll let you."

We're jammed at the penthouse door, and I do not want to leave this suite when everything I've ever needed is already in my grasp.

Nicole pauses, tipping her head as she tries to read me. "What are you thinking?"

"How happy I'm going to make the two of you." Is my voice extra raspy right now? Huh. Is that what emotions and feelings do to it? It's not too bad, honestly. "I'm never going to let anything happen to either of you."

"We know," Landon and Nicole say at the same time. Then they start laughing.

"Okay, wow. Who are you and what have you done with Kerrington-can't-show-his-emotions-ever? You know, the man I'm in love with? Because you, stranger..." Landon drags his gaze up and down my locked in body. "Well, you're pretty hot soooo."

It feels like I've busted into a billion happy cells.

"I fucking love you." Smacking Landon's ass, I signal him to move out first. "And I fucking love you too." I spank Nicole twice for good measure.

We leave the hotel with our hands clasped and future bright.

I waited a long time to feel this complete. I think we all have.

And now there's nothing left to stand in our way from embracing the best life ever. Together.

Epilogue

Nicole

"Thank you, so much for your support over the years. I wish you all happiness and success always."

Cameras flash and a roar of questions fly my way, but I ignore them all and step off the podium. Kerrington is on my left, Landon's on my right, and I clasp both their hands and let them escort me off the stage.

I just gave my final speech as a member of the Greystone Foundation. As of this moment, I'm just Nicole with no job and a hella hot set of boyfriends.

Can life get any sweeter? Doubtful.

Snow is in tonight's forecast here in New York and it's got me in the mood for fireplace sex. We're staying at my place until after the holidays because my mom wasn't kidding about seeing my guys for Christmas. She's already called Kerrington twice and Landon three times verifying their favorite dishes so the cook can have them at dinner.

Leah is joining us, too. So of course, Mason

is coming. Ugh. I can't shake that guy at all. Stalker.

Just kidding. I'll gladly put up with Mase if it means I get to go shopping with Leah. She's a gem and definitely a bestie. Speaking of besties… I've called Grace and told her everything. She was annoyed about me keeping the whole Tim thing from her, but understood why. She was also super supportive and excited for me, because of course she's been team Double Trouble all along. That's what she calls my guys.

She's not wrong.

"Nicole! Can you tell us what your next plans are now that you're no longer the face of the Greystone Foundation?" a reporter shouts, stepping in my way.

I feel Kerrington tense up and I squeeze his hand, letting him know it's okay. The last thing I want is for him to attack this poor guy who's just trying to do his job.

"I'm going to buy a house, a minivan, and live a happy life." *There. Put that in your article and see how many clicks the truth gets you.*

I'm so glad I've broken free from the drama of my toxic social circles and the expectations of others.

My only job, according to Landon, is to make myself happy from here on out.

It'll be my best career yet.

That's not to say I'm giving up fundraising entirely though. Already my mind's racing with new ideas to help others and raise awareness about certain topics I hold near and dear to me. We'll see what I start up next.

Funny, I can't make a business for myself like Mason and the guys did. But I'm damn good at helping others. I can raise money faster than I can make it. I know, I know, I'm a mathematical mystery. Landon says it's because my passion is in helping others, not getting rich, which, he also clarified, is his passion.

He's still on a hunt for an island and has it narrowed down to two and can't choose.

Kerrington told him to buy both.

I swear I have no idea what I'm going to do with these two.

"You ready to go home, Duchess?" Kerrington pauses at the end of the sidewalk and opens my car door for me.

I slip inside and he shuts the door. Landon gets in the back, smiling like a cheshire cat.

That's suspicious. "What are you two up to?"

"Nothing."

Nothing my ass. Landon's smile is even bigger now.

"What's going on, guys?"

Kerrington shuts his door and starts the engine. "Nothing's going on."

"Liar." I don't like feeling left out, but it's obvious they're not doing it to be mean. "Give me a clue?"

"Nope." Kerrington shoves his finger at Landon. "Don't break and give her one."

"What? Psht. I would never."

I beg, guess, and ask questions for a solid twenty minutes as we fight through Manhattan traffic. Landon stays strong the whole ride and Kerrington's a brick wall.

By the time we pull up to my home, I'm annoyed. "Fine. Don't tell me." I storm past them and practically shove my key into the lock, chipping a nail.

The door opens and I walk into a living room filled with candles, roses, and a lit fireplace. My anger melts instantly because I wasn't really mad to begin with.

"Aww, you guys." I spin around and freeze.

They're both on their knees. And they're both holding rings out to me.

I take a step back.

"We know you're against marriage," Landon says. "But we still want you to be ours."

"I hardly need a ring to be yours." My heart gallops in my chest. Tears sting my eyes. I've always been adamant about not wanting to get married to anyone, but that was only because my marriage wasn't going to be my choice. This is different.

"We're not asking for marriage. We're asking for you to choose," Kerrington says.

I shake my head. There's no way in Hell I could ever choose between them.

"Choose *us*," Landon says, reading my mind.

Kerrington's brow pinches, as if he's afraid I'll run again. "Give us the honor of spending the rest of our lives making you happy."

"We won't make you regret it," Landon adds.

As if I could ever regret a single moment I've had with these two? Impossible.

"We're so proud of you, baby. Taking control of your life, knowing your worth, going after what you want." Kerrington's voice does this straining, raspy thing that happens when he gets too emotional. It pulls my heart strings big time. "We just want to be part of it forever."

"And a ring will do that?"

Landon side-eyes Kerrington. "I told you handcuffing her to us was a more logical option."

"Shut up."

The way I break out into a giggle fit is something I'll never live down. "Oh my god, you two." I sink to my knees in front of them and wrap them in my arms. "You're going to drive me crazy."

"I mean, you say that like it's a bad thing." Landon wraps his arms around me and beams.

Kerrington shrugs playfully. "I like you crazy. You're fun when you're unhinged."

That makes me laugh even harder.

"Yes."

Landon looks at Kerrington. "Did she say

yes to us or…. Am I being delulu?"

"Say it again, Duchess."

"Yes," I repeat, locking gazes with Kerrington. "Yes, yes, yes."

"She definitely said yes," Landon whispers loudly at him. Then he fists bumps the air. "Wait. Does this mean you're wearing the rings, or should I order new handcuffs?"

We broke the last two sets being too rough last week.

"Collar, leash, handcuffs, rings, I want it all."

My guys light up. "We're soooo buying a house with a basement, Kerr."

They break out in belly laughs, but I'm at a loss. "I don't get it."

"We'll tell you later." Kerrington slips his ring on my left hand while Landon slides his onto my right.

Gasping, it hits me. "Oh my god. Are you working on a kidnapping fantasy? Because if so, I'm totally down for that. Tie me up, Daddy."

"Aaaand I'm done." Landon stands up and tosses his hands in the air. "I swear I never met a more perfect woman than you and the fact that you're this unhinged really fucks with my head."

"Good. Now let me fuck with your other head." I grab him by the belt and yank him against me.

"Fuuuuck." He closes his eyes, already in bliss.

"Happy wife, happy life," Kerrington recites, stripping our man down with me.

Then we take turns breaking each other's control, screaming one another's names, and worshipping the love that has been building between us for a very long time. The one that was out of our reach for so long. The love that almost passed us by.

The one I had to break free from my chains and run to.

And I'm never looking back.

OTHER BOOKS
BY THIS AUTHOR

For information on this book, other books in my
backlist, and future releases,
please visit: **www.BrianaMichaels.com**

If you liked this book, please help spread the
word by leaving a review on the site you
purchased your copy, or on a reader site such as
Goodreads.

I'd love to hear from readers too, so feel free to
send me an email at:
Briana@BrianaMichaels.com
or visit me on Facebook:
www.facebook.com/BrianaMichaelsAuthor

Thank you!

ABOUT THE AUTHOR

Briana Michaels grew up and still lives on the East Coast. When taking a break from the crazy adventures in her head, she enjoys running around with her two children. If there is time to spare, she loves to read, cook, hike in the woods, and sit outside by a roaring fire. She does all of this with the love and support of her amazing husband who always has her back, encouraging her to go for her dreams. Aye, she's a lucky girl indeed.

www.ingramcontent.com/pod-product-compliance
Lightning Source LLC
Chambersburg PA
CBHW071535110726
47908CB00007B/1890